OPPOSITION

AN ENEMIES TO LOVERS ROMANCE (NYC DOMS)

JANE HENRY

Opposition: An Enemies to Lovers Romance (NYC Doms)

by Jane Henry

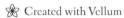 Created with Vellum

ONE

Cora

"IT'S the *justice* of the situation, Chandra," I tell her, while I push the button to grind the coffee beans. The fragrant aroma makes my stomach growl with hunger, which doesn't even make logical sense because you don't even eat coffee. "The separation of the classes in this city is just utterly *maddening*."

"I agree, honey," Chandra says, waddling over to me with a large sleeve of paper cups. Chandra's hugely pregnant and ready to pop. We met in college a few years ago and became fast friends, so when my life imploded a few months ago, Chandra was the one who got me the job here at Books and Cups. Petite, with dark, coffee-colored skin and vibrant brown eyes, Chandra is beautiful. Pregnancy becomes her, as she's grown pleasantly plump and fairly glows. Leaning against the counter, she rests a hand on the enormous bulge of her abdomen and giggles. "And apparently, the baby does, too."

"Awww," I say. "Is she kicking again?"

"*He.*" Axle's growly voice comes from the doorway as he makes his way into the shop. Chandra and Axle haven't figured out the sex of their baby, and it's become a point of contention between us. I insist Chandra's having a girl, mostly just to irk her husband, and Axle insists he's having a son, mostly just to provoke Chandra. I really don't care either way, but it's fun to tease them.

"And what is the injustice we're fighting today, Cora?" Axle bends down to brush a kiss to Chandra's cheek, and I watch them with a sort of wistful hopefulness. They represent everything I want in life. After years apart from one another, they found each other again, overcoming so many obstacles to forge their way back into each other's lives. Now they're preparing to raise a family in the heart of the city. She adores the ground he walks on, and he dotes on her. She's my friend, so I know it isn't always sunshine and roses, and they have their moments like everyone else.

"The Greenery, Axle," I tell him, my heartbeat accelerating as I take up my cause once more. "They want to pave over The Greenery because they're building some other stupid high-rise. Because *that's* what this city needs is another *high-rise.*"

"Who does?" he asks.

"Oh, who knows," I tell him. I've only just begun research today, but as I'm studying investigative reporting at school, and I have a major paper on this subject due by the end of the month, I'll do my research tonight.

After I finish my job at Books and Cups.

And make sure Ben and Bailey have done their homework and gone to bed.

And picked up some food at the twenty-four-hour supermarket on the way home.

After this, I've got a second job Chandra and Marla got me a few months ago, at Club Verge. Marla's the bookstore owner and a long-term member of Club Verge. Chandra and Axle are members, too. At first, they were all hesitant to even talk to me about it, but there's a reason I'm drawn to Marla's bookstore. She stocks the largest selection of kinky romance in the city, and hell, I love those books.

So even though I'm not in the lifestyle... and I have *no desire* to be... I'm pretty open-minded. And hell, the other bartender, Travis, is cute and sweet.

My phone rings, and Chandra nods for me to take it when I show her the screen. We're not supposed to talk on the phone when we're on a shift, but bookstore owner Marla understands my circumstances are different. When I see it's Bailey, I take the call.

"What is it?" I ask, turning my back to the counter and whispering into the phone. "Everything okay?"

"Yeah," Bailey says. "I'm really sorry to bug you at work, Cora. I know you're not supposed to take calls."

"It's okay," I say quickly. "Why'd you call?"

"Yeah," she says. "But I... well, I don't know what to feed Ben for dinner." She sighs.

I pinch the bridge of my nose with my thumb and index finger and lower my voice. I don't like even my closest friends to know the reality of our situation. They all know I'm guardian to my two youngest siblings. That I fought the system and won, when my mother was put in jail for larceny and driving under the influence and my younger siblings were in danger of being tossed into the NYC foster care system. That I'm the one holding it together after she overdosed in prison and I'm left with two minors under my care. What they don't know is that I barely make enough money to pay for the tiny apartment we live in. I need to stay in school if I'm ever going to get a better-paying job, and that means my jobs are limited.

Our cupboards are so bare, it makes me want to cry. Hell, I *have* cried. I've had nothing but a stale muffin all day long, and only because Marla was going to discard it because it wasn't fresh anymore.

I played it off like I was making an environmentally-conscious decision, and Marla might've bought it, but the truth was, we were totally out of food and I was starving. And now I feel guilty for eating a stupid stale muffin.

"There's a box of mac and cheese in the cabinet," I tell her. "I know there is." It's barely enough for the two of them, but it'll do. They get free breakfast and lunch at school, thanks to the generosity of the NYC school system, but dinner's another story.

"Yeah," she says with a sigh. "But the little bit of milk we have left is bad, and there's no butter."

Fuck.

"I'm sorry, honey," I say.

Someone clears their throat behind me, and I quickly swivel around. From where I'm standing, I can see there's a man in a suit drumming his fingers on the glass countertop, but I can't see much else. Damn it. Chandra's three aisles over helping another customer. It's just me here.

"Just a minute, Bailey," I say, walking back over to the counter.

I look up... and up... and up.

This man's huge. So tall and so broad, he'd look like a linebacker for the Jets if he wasn't dressed in a suit that looks like it costs my yearly wages. But it isn't just his height and breadth that makes my stomach tighten when I look at him. It isn't the clench of his strong, chiseled jaw. Or the sapphire blue eyes that pierce right through me with utter disdain.

It's that he's fucking *glaring* at me, his lips pinched together like he's just tasted something bad. I can't decide if I want to apologize or slap him.

"Sorry to interrupt your conversation with your boyfriend," he says, his tone riddled with disdain, and *God,* his voice sounds like sex. Deep and smooth, like gourmet chocolate.

Wait. Hold the phone.

Boyfriend?

"But I'd like to order a cup of coffee sometime today," he finishes with a scowl. "Do you think you can tear yourself away long enough to fill that order?"

"Excuse me?"

What the hell?

"Coffee," he repeats, then makes a pouring motion with his hand and air-sips the pretend cup. Flicking his wrist, he looks at his obnoxious gold Rolex. "*Today?*"

To my surprise, there's a tattoo that peaks under the bright white cuff of his shirt and it catches me off guard. Everything else about him seems so highbrow and conservative.

Whatever.

Like I give a shit.

"Yes, of course," I tell him through gritted teeth. "I'll be right with you."

I turn my back to him and can swear I *feel* him

seething from where I stand. My cheeks flame. *Damn* my fair, pale skin. He'll see my pink cheeks and for some reason, I hate that.

"Bailey," I whisper into the phone. "I'm sorry, babe, you'll have to use water."

She sighs. "Okay. Can you pick something up tonight?"

"Yes," I tell her. "I promise." Marla will give me my tips before I leave, and that'll be enough for at least a few things. "I gotta go."

We hang up and I square my shoulders to face the man at the counter. *King Douchebag.*

Most of the customers who come in here are pretty decent. We have our regulars, and many of Club Verge members come in here on occasion. But it's NYC, and we also have our fair share of jerks.

"What can I get you, sir?"

I glare right back at the beautiful bastard with my hands on my hips, but at first, he doesn't answer. Instead, he drags his gaze from my eyes to my collarbone, then lower, lingering on my cleavage. Figures, the one good thing my mama gave me was a decent set of boobs, but now I wish I was wearing a bulky sweater, and not this thin little V-neck top. But laundry day is Saturday, and the laundromat costs a *lot* of money, so I try to wear things a few times, and my clothing options are really limited.

He doesn't stop there, though but lets his gaze roam over my softly-rounded tummy, the hands placed on my full hips, then once he's given me a painfully slow once-over, he goes all the way back up to the top again until he finally meets my eyes. I'm so shocked by his bold perusal of my body my mouth drops open. I clamp it shut when I realize he's smirking at me.

Yeah, I've made up my mind about him alright.

I want to slap him.

"Please," he drawls, in that sexy-as-sin voice. "The largest cup of coffee you have."

"Cream or sugar?"

"No. Black."

Of course.

I turn to pour him his cup of coffee when I realize the light's off on the thing.

Shit. One of us must've hit the breaker by accident.

"Just a minute," I tell him. "Unfortunately, it looks like our machine's unplugged. I'll have to make you another pot."

He sighs with exasperation.

"Excellent. I'll just wait here, then."

"Why don't you do that," I mutter. I keep my back to him, and hear footsteps approaching. Marla's making her way to us from the back room, her hair tied up in a ponytail, nose smudged with dust. She was likely doing inventory and came to check on the front end.

Marla's a few years older than I am, with light brown hair and eyes, and a pair of slim glasses perched on her nose. She's not only the bookstore owner, she's become a friend to me, like an older sister, and I hate that she caught me at a bad time like this. I enjoy when she's pleased with the work that I've done. And now...

"Hey, Cora!" she says cheerfully, then turns to face the stranger. "Oh, hello. Are you being helped?"

"Theoretically," he mutters. I watch as Marla's eyes widen, and she looks at me in surprise.

My chest tightens and tears prick my eyes. It matters to me to do a good job, and I dislike the insinuation that I'm not. Worse, I hate crying in front of people. Internalizing my anger makes me emotional, and I fucking hate that.

Marla shoots me a look of sympathy and leans in to whisper, "Honey, go take a break. I'll handle this guy."

I shake my head. Nope. I'm not gonna let him chase me off.

"I'm good, thank you." She raises a brow, so I continue, "I can do this, Marla."

Stepping a little closer to me, she whispers in my ear, "Of course you can. He just doesn't seem super... *pleasant*. You sure?"

I nod. "So sure."

"Interesting selection of books you have," the man says, leaning against the counter and glancing at the titles on display. Marla takes pride in her eclectic little shop.

"Thank you," she says. "Several were written by friends of mine, actually." Chandra and Marla's friend Giada both write kinky romance books and have quite a following of dedicated readers. We actually had a signing last month, and the line went all the way out the door for *hours*.

He shakes his head with a frown and a rueful chuckle. "What an excellent waste of time those books are."

I've had enough of this asshole's crap. I pour him the now-steaming coffee and hand it to him.

"What is and what is not a waste of time is totally relative," I tell him. "For your information, those books provide endless hours of entertainment, and they're written by excellent writers."

Taking the coffee from my hand, he passes me a twenty-dollar bill.

"Entertainment?" he scoffs. He pierces me with a look while I fetch his change. "Books are meant to educate, yet those books are doing nothing of the sort. They make men into mythical creatures and women to be hapless victims. And worst of all? They glorify the BDSM scene with no real-world knowledge." He shakes his head.

I open my mouth to protest but Marla shakes her head. Instead, I gather his change with tight lips, biting back every retort.

"Keep the change, Cora," he says.

And then he's gone. I stand with a stack of bills in my hand.

"He seems familiar," Marla murmurs. "But I don't think I've ever seen him in here before. Have you?" Quietly she takes the bills from my hand, folds them, and places them in my pocket. "I'll get the rest of your tips to you before you go."

"Thanks," I tell her. A part of me wants to take his stupid money and throw it at him, but... well, I've got mouths to feed. I don't have the luxury of pride. "And no. I don't think I've ever seen him before. And frankly? I'll be happy if I never see him again."

WHEN I FINISH up my shift, I take my backpack and sling it over my shoulder, then head to Verge. Even though I'm still unsettled with the whole interaction between me and the jerk, I'm looking forward to going to Verge. I love the people there. I have only a few close friends, and they're all as busy as I am, and even though it's a little weird to admit, the people at Verge have become like a second family to me.

I huff out a quiet laugh to myself. Figures, I'd find a second family at a sex club. BDSM Club. Whatever it is. But there's something about that kinky crowd that I love... the way they're free to be their quirky, crazy selves without fear of judgment or ridicule. And the feminist in me applauds the pursuit of sexual freedom. It's partly why I love Marla's store.

The lonely widow, snarky school teacher, harried stay-at-home mom. The powerful Wall Street executives, fearless leaders, intellectual visionaries. All of them are free to live out their fantasies in the pages of a book. And everyone needs a little escapism. Club Verge, to me, is kinda the same thing.

Braxton stands as bouncer to the door tonight. Tall and broad with a ready grin and sharp tongue, he's one of my faves. His girl Zoe is feisty as hell, and a member of the NYC Police force.

"Hi, Brax," I say brightly, as he holds open the massive black door to Verge so I can step inside.

"Cora. How you been, kiddo?" I haven't seen him in a few days, and he acts like he's missed me.

Something inside me warms despite the whole *kiddo* thing.

"Good. Working my ass off at school and stuff. The usual," I say, and he gives me a sympathetic nod. "Zoe here tonight?"

"Nah. She's got an overnight shift. I saw Diana and Beatrice head in a little while ago, though. I think Giada, too." He rolls his eyes. "Not like anyone can tell, though." He looks over his shoulder to make sure no one hears him. "Stupidest idea ever, to have a masquerade party like we're some kinda fuckin' sorority."

I groan. I totally forgot tonight was Masquerade night at Verge. I'm told they don't do holiday parties, but their competition apparently does, so this year Verge has decided to begin occasional themed nights.

"So people are wearing masks and stuff?" I ask him. It's not uncommon for people who go to sex clubs to wear masks, but somehow knowing most people will be makes me a little uneasy.

"You could say that," he says, but then he turns to face a couple entering behind me, so I wave good-bye and head into the club.

Club Verge is large and sprawling, clean and well lit. Current club owners, husband and wife, Tobias and Diana Creed, make sure to keep Verge classy by vetting members and enforcing strict adherence to basic rules. It helps that the most prominent members and dungeon monitors are long-term members of Verge, and several are officers for the NYPD.

Right beyond the entryway sits Tobias' office to my right, and to the left, a lobby outfitted with comfortable furniture and paperwork. Contracts and the like are available for members to negotiate terms of play before they enter. It's not required, as some are long-term couples and others are just here to observe, but new partners looking to scene are encouraged to lay down the ground rules before they begin. Tonight, though, the lobby is vacant.

Beyond the lobby is the entrance to the main bar area, and my place of business. The doorway opens to a massive floor. The gleaming bar with bar stools and bright overhead lighting that makes the glasses sparkle sits to the left, and to the right are small, round tables for members to sit together. Beyond that lies the pool tables and dance floor. This is the fun part, and where I spend most of my time, as people party and mingle and socialize. Just beyond this room, though, lies the area of Club Verge that piques my interest. I just haven't been brave enough to venture there beyond my initial brief tour.

Down the hall is the dungeon... with every BDSM accoutrement one could hope for. And down the hall from the dungeon are all the private rooms for long-term members. The doors are color-coded and locked. I've never seen one, though they interest me.

That's where the *real* fun happens. Or so I imagine.

I wouldn't know.

I... hear things. See things.

And hell, I want to know more. But who has time for things like relationships? I'm a full-time college student and legal guardian to my younger brother and sister. And God, if Child Protective Services ever heard that I was involved in a kinky scene in a club, I can't imagine what they'd do with that. It's much safer for me here at the bar.

So much safer.

I place my bag in a locker in the small employee room near Tobias' office. I eye the vending machines with envy, my stomach aching with hunger. That muffin seems like a long, long time ago.

I bite my lip. The cash in my pocket weighs heavily. It isn't much, but hell I need it. Figures we live in one of the most expensive cities ever. We pay twice as much for basic groceries than the national average. I feel a little dizzy when I turn away from the machine and put on one of the clean aprons that hangs on a hook. We serve warmed mixed nuts at the bar, and employees are free to help themselves. That'll tide me over.

I enter the bar area and can't help but smile. Travis, who hails from Texas, stands at the bar dressed in full cowboy attire. He shoots me a boyish grin and tips his hat to me when I take my place behind the bar.

"Howdy," I say with a snicker. He's wearing worn leather jeans, a wide leather belt with one of those massive oval metal buckles, cowboy boots, a bandana or something tied around his neck, and a large, tan-colored Stetson.

"Howdy, purdy lady," he says. I groan.

"You hit your older brother up for some..." I pause, searching for the right word. "*Gitup?*"

I giggle when he swats at me with a dishtowel.

"Supposed to be fancy dress night," he drawls, shaking his head at me. "You didn't get the memo?"

I stick my tongue out at him. "I have work to do, cowboy."

"Hey, Cora." I look up to see Diana and Beatrice approaching the bar. At least I think it's Beatrice, as she's dressed from head to toe in black leather in a Catwoman costume, whip and all. Diana's one of my favorite people here, tall and graceful with long, super curly hair and kind eyes. I grin at her. She's wearing a full-on Wonder Woman costume.

"You look awesome. Is that... Beatrice under all that black leather? Catwoman or Dominatrix?" She's tiny, but tonight she's wearing platform boots and carrying a scary-looking leather whip.

"Dominatrix my ass," comes a growly voice to my left. Beatrice's husband Zack, wearing just civilian clothing and a scowl, takes her by the elbow and draws her to him. "Remember what I said about that whip, woman." He's her long-term dominant, and one of the more serious guys around here. Pulling her close, he kisses her, then when he's got her disarmed, he nimbly flicks the whip out of her hand.

"I'll take that," he says.

"Zack! You fooled me!" Beatrice playfully smacks his chest.

"Watch it," he says, shaking his head and coiling the whip in his hand. "Lest you forget. I'm experienced in relieving people of their weapons."

"He's just jealous he doesn't look half as good as you," Diana teases, taking a glass of wine that Travis hands her.

"Yeah, that's it," Zack says, rolling his eyes. "Did you get something to eat yet?" he asks Beatrice. "They've got food over by the pool tables tonight."

My stomach aches.

"Since when?" I say, trying to pretend like I'm not starving and just curious why they're serving food.

"Well," Diana says, taking a seat at the bar. "A

few months back, we asked for member feedback, and lots of people wanted more food so they could stay longer, so we decided on our themed nights we'd have some tables set up in there. The problem is, people keep trying to sneak food in the dungeon, and that's not happening."

"Why not?" I ask. I have no idea what goes on in the dungeon, and I wonder what the reasoning is.

Beatrice giggles and Travis walks over to me. "There's sex in there," he says with a grin. "Bodily fluids? May not be okay with the NYC health department."

"Oh, ew," I say without thinking, wrinkling up my nose.

"Well," Beatrice says. "Don't *ew* it until you've tried it." She bites her lip when she looks at Zack, who responds by giving her a flick of the whip. Squealing, she comes up on her toes, and I instantly feel my body heat from the sound of the crack.

"I just meant... about the *food,* not the... well... public sex." My damn cheeks flame, so red, they likely match my hair, as if they all know my breasts are swelling and a pulse of arousal just flared between my legs.

God.

I've been watching people interact here for months, reading every book I can at Marla's, and telling myself this isn't for me. But somehow that flick of the whip did strange, erotic things to my body. What the hell?

A few customers place drink orders, and I get busy filling them. I need to eat something, though. It doesn't usually affect me like this, but I'm so hungry I can barely think straight. I'm handing a gin and tonic to a girl wearing a slinky mermaid gown, when I feel someone staring at me. The hair on the back of my neck prickles and I glance around the room. It takes me a minute until I see him, and when I do, I nearly drop the drink.

Standing against the dungeon door, he takes up the whole door frame with his massive height and breadth. He's wearing nothing but head-to-toe black and a mask that covers his eyes and nose. It takes me a minute to realize he's in a mime's costume, yet his shirt is sleeveless, showing strong, muscled arms covered in tattoos. Like a sexy sorta twist on an age-old classic. Mute. Powerful. Cloaked in mystery. I want to see all of him. And why is he staring at me?

"Who is that?" I ask Beatrice on a whisper. I lift my finger to point, but before she turns to look, he crooks a finger at me. I blink. Once more, he beckons, then turns around and walks straight into the dungeon. He's more than a mime. He's a puppeteer, because I feel the tug like I'm attached to him when he walks away, like I need to follow him. To somehow satisfy an unknown hunger in me that's as powerful as physical starvation.

"I don't know who he is," Beatrice whispers back. "Not sure I've seen him before. But, babe? If it were *me*? I'd go."

"Go where?" Diana chirps up.

"The dungeon," Beatrice says, filling her in quickly.

Diana gives me a grin. "Isn't it around your break time?"

TWO

Liam

I ALMOST DIDN'T COME HERE TONIGHT. Though I always come here wearing a mask, I'm not into the whole juvenile "fancy dress" bullshit, but when I remembered I had a mime costume in the back of my work closet from the last time I did this under duress, I decided I'd do it. I work too damn hard, and the only reprieve I get is when I'm working out or at Club Verge.

Club Verge is exactly thirty-two minutes from my Manhattan office. When I relocated here from my Boston office, I was pleased to find out an old friend of mine opened this place. Tobias and I were both members of a Club in Boston a full decade ago, and though we parted ways, we were good friends back then. He took me in, gave me a private room since he knows me, and I like how he runs this place. Tobias and his small, dedicated staff have protected my identity. They keep this place tight, running heavy security and vetting every single member who comes in here. I like it here. When I step through that black door, I'm no longer Liam Alexander, Wall Street executive and C.E.O. of Alexander Enterprises.

I'm simply *master*.

There are many beautiful, fetching women here who easily succumb to my mastery over them. Few who are looking for a full-time relationship, and that suits me well. I like to leave my identity at the door and assume the role of anonymous master when I'm here. No one knows my net worth. No one disgusts me with their cloying attention. No one panders to me, hoping for some sort of payout.

But then I saw her... the beautiful brat from the bookstore. I don't know what came over me, as I wasn't planning on picking anyone up tonight. But when I saw the way she leaned against the bar with her hands wrapped around her waist, a classic sign of vulnerability and fear... when I saw the way she looked at me with wide eyes, her mouth parted... I had to have her.

She doesn't know who I am.

And I plan on keeping it that way.

At first, I feared she wouldn't come, and stood in the shadow of the doorway to watch. When her friend whispered in her ear, she nodded. Diana, her boss, gave a nod. And now she's coming my way.

I have no idea what I'm going to do with her when I see her. This isn't like me. I like things orderly and planned. Routinized. I'm hardly spontaneous. But this girl... this girl with her fiery red hair and cliché temper to match, she does something to me.

I provoked her in the bookstore earlier. I have little patience for poor service, but something told me she had good reason. I wasn't really annoyed at her. I wanted to see how she'd behave if I toyed with her. Would she crumple and cow to me like every other woman I see?

Or would she fight me?

Yeah. I know I'm a bastard.

When I saw her pale, freckled skin heat with anger, the pink tone made me want to draw my tongue along that fragile, gorgeous collarbone of hers. When her eyes flashed at me, I imagined capturing her slim wrists in my hands, pinning them against that counter, and slamming my palm against her full ass until those beautiful eyes brimmed with tears.

I like to cause pain... of a certain type.

I like to make them cry then kiss it better.

I've seen her at the bar, but she didn't really catch my attention before now. She's always so busy, so distracted. Travis knows me, so he's the one I order drinks from. And until today, I figured she was just some kid looking to make an extra buck.

I didn't know her eyes were a delicate robin's

egg blue, wide and rimmed in impossibly long lashes.

I didn't know her skin was as pale as fine porcelain, dotted with fetching freckles. I want to count every one of them, especially the ones hidden from me.

I didn't know her flaming red hair begged to be wrapped around my fingers. I want to tug her head back until that gorgeous mouth of hers falls open and capture her full lips between my teeth.

I want to defile her. Overpower her. Dominate her.

But first, I need to seduce her.

Before she even steps foot in the dungeon, I know I'm making a mistake. I want to become a long-term member here, so I have be careful. Taking advantage of one of Verge's employees is a dumbass move, and not one that I should make.

I can have a little fun, though.

Will it be so easy? To beckon to her? And have her submit to me?

I wait by the doorway to see if she'll come, and when I see her coming my way, I can't help but smile. Her head is tipped to the side, as if she's curious. Without a word, I extend my hand. I fully intend on making the most of being a mime for the night.

"Hi," she says awkwardly, a pretty pink coloring her cheeks once more. Lifting her hand, she wiggles her little fingers at me. I take her hand in mine and bow, greeting her in silence.

"Mimes don't... um... talk, right?"

I shake my head no, then lead her inside the dungeon. But as soon as we set foot in the room, she tenses, and I can feel her resisting. I turn to give her a quizzical look.

"I—I've never been in the dungeon before," she tells me. "I have no idea what's going on."

I nod, then point to a vacant loveseat.

"Okay," she says hesitantly. I sit down on one end, and wordlessly tug her onto my lap. Her whole body tenses, but she doesn't pull away. Instead, she sits primly with her hands on her lap. I enjoy watching the flush of her cheeks deepen. When her beautiful eyes go wide, I point to the sign above us, a large red delicious apple with the bold word **APPLE** below it. Beneath the word, the caption reads *Club Safeword.*

I'm told for safety reasons the Club administration took it upon themselves to issue a universal club safeword. Originally it was *Big Apple,* in honor of the city's nickname. But they shortened it to apple, and now every room in the Club has a sign reminding members. I've never heard it used, but it's a convenient safety net for tonight. If I'm a mime, I can't negotiate a safeword.

"That's the club safeword," she says. "You want me to... use it if I need it?" She breathes a little more heavily. We both know why she'd need to safeword.

I nod. Looking from me to the sign, then back to me again, she finally swallows, then nods.

"Okay," she says. "I've never done anything like this before. I'm not a—I don't know. Bottom? Submissive? I just... I mean I've read about them, but..."

I place my finger to her lips.

No more chatter, little girl.

When my skin touches hers, she shivers.

Perfect.

The girl deserves to be punished for her behavior today. Even if I did test her limits, she should know better than to chat with her boyfriend instead of serving coffee to loyal customers.

I left her a tip, but only so she'd see that I could.

Dragging my thumb along the apple of her cheek, I let my silent touch speak for me. I want to explore her whole body, until she's trembling with need. When I gently drag my touch along the thin skin at her collarbone, I can feel her pulse racing, the heat of it making my dick hard. If she feels my erection under her ass, she doesn't let on, but lets me touch her. After a few minutes of the gentle caresses—fingers at the edge of her hair, fingertips to the temples, the lightest of touches along her shoulder to her elbow—she begins to relax.

I open my mouth to tell her she's a good girl when I remember that I'm silent tonight. Instead I nod, which seems to please her.

Without a word, I point to several items around us. A spanking bench. Horse. St. Andrew's Cross. I leave out the stocks and exam table, the harnesses and electric play equipment, not because I'm not into that sort of thing... but if this is her first time, I want to be easy on her.

Every time I point to something, she turns her head to look at me, and shakes it a little.

"No," she says, at the sight of someone strapped to the cross. "No way."

I take the top of her hand and point back to the sign above my head.

"Right," she says. "But I don't need to safeword *yet,* right?"

I nod.

"Only if I need," she continues. "Still... no. I don't want... that."

What *does* she want? She's said no to everything. I wonder why she came in here at all.

I'm beginning to think she wants nothing and is just here to observe, when we see Zack and Beatrice come in. She's wearing his collar and chain, and he's got a firm grip on it. On hands and knees, she follows him, but he's slow and careful while they walk. As if they're the only couple in the room, he leans down and whispers in her ear.

Cora stills.

Sitting down on a loveseat, he pats his knee, and Beatrice bends over his leg eagerly. She wants a spanking. Shaking his head with a chuckle, he swats her ass hard with his palm. Once. Twice. Three times. Beatrice moans when Zack leans down and whispers something in her ear before he gives her a few more sharp spanks. She molds to his lap as if she's meant to be there, and it's clear they've done this a time or two. It's a tame spanking, and over-the-lap isn't really my thing. But still... my cock strains beneath Cora's ass when Beatrice moans, clearly aroused by the spanking, and she turns to look at me. To my surprise, she nods, her cheeks flushed.

I point to the couple and raise my brows.

This? Is this what you want?

Biting her lip, she nods, then to my surprise pushes herself off my knee and flops belly down over my lap, like she wants to do this before she loses her resolve.

"Is this okay?" She asks, too quickly, her nerves getting the best of her. "Am I... should I... gah, I don't even know what to ask. But yes. Yes, I know that if I don't like what you're doing, to safeword."

Gently, I place my finger to her lips to get her to stop her incessant chatter.

Shaking her head, she goes on.

"Just a few smacks," she says. "Oh, *God,* do you even *call* it that? I'm just curious is all."

Whack.

"*Oh!*"

I take her by surprise when I smack her beautiful ass hard with my palm. So she wants a spanking. I don't need to be asked twice. I've wanted to punish her since she threw sass at me in the bookstore, so the tingle in my palm is immensely satisfying. I swallow hard. Jesus, I love this.

In one fluid motion, I capture her wrists and bring them to the small of her back, before I deliver a second sharp spank. She tenses when I spank her but doesn't say anything. I glide my hand along the curve of her ass, feeling the heat straight through to my palm, until I get to the tops of her thighs, then drag my palm across her full ass again. Lifting my palm, I spank her again, harder this time, then soothe the sting with firm strokes of my palm. A slow, over-the-knee hand spanking is probably the tamest thing we could do here, and maybe that's why this is where she wants to start. But it's also immediately intimate, and I wonder about that.

After a pattern of spanks and caresses, I gently part her thighs with the back of my hand. She tenses but doesn't protest when I drag my fingers between her legs. I rub the fabric at her slit, firmly, loving the way her breathing accelerates. Christ, she's gorgeous.

I withdraw my hand and spank her again, then smooth out the pain, then I raise my hand and give her another smack before I drag my fingers to her clothed pussy again. I build a rhythm of pain and pleasure until she's writhing on my knee, her breath coming in little, panting gasps.

I spank her for mouthing off, for shooting those beautiful eyes of hers at me with accusation. For sparring with me so rudely I won't be able to set foot in that store again without imagining this, right now, right here, this gorgeous redhead sprawled over my lap getting her ass spanked. I spank her for being foolish enough to follow the beckon of a stranger. I could be a masked murderer for all she knows, and here she is under my control.

Smack.

I've heard some women can come from just a spanking, though I've never seen one, and as our session continues, I wonder if Cora is one of them. I can tell every slap of my palm brings her closer and closer. She's gasping, panting, and ready to come.

I toy with the idea of bringing her to the edge then leaving her there, because I'm a controlling fucking bastard and I can teach her a lesson in ways she doesn't expect... but I need to see her chase her climax. I need to see how beautiful she looks when I bring her to the edge of utter bliss.

When her ass is hot to the touch even through her clothes, her eyes closed, and her lips parted, I spread her thighs apart again with the back of my hand and hold her in place. Slowly, with painstaking care, I glide my fingers between her thighs again.

"I'm going to—oh, God—I can't—"

Without use of my words, I have to encourage her with my touch. Smoothing the damp hair from her forehead, I tuck it behind her ear and run the back of my finger along her cheek, then ghost my index finger across her lips to silence her. Sighing, she slumps over my lap and bucks her hips. I smile to myself. She'll likely regret this later.

I won't.

I stroke harder, faster, relishing every little gasp and moan, until she keens with pleasure and loses her mind. Half-crying, gasping, she groans with exquisite beauty as she climaxes hard over my lap. "Oh, God," she chokes, her voice rising in pitch, as I help her ride her pleasure. I stroke her to completion as she comes with abandon. In that moment, this isn't about revenge or my own self pleasure. In that moment, I want to give her the best fucking orgasm of her life. I want her replaying her lust-filled night with a stranger in her mind over. And over. And over.

When she finally slumps over my lap, I spread my legs and let her fall to the floor in front of me. Her sex-sated eyes meet mine and she squirms a bit. Does she recognize me? If she does, she doesn't let on. Her gaze registers the barest sign of recognition, then she shakes her head, as if to mentally dismiss whatever reservations she has.

I point one final time to the sign above my head as I unfasten my buckle. There's no fear in the beautiful depths of her eyes, though. Her gaze bright and eager. I have a private room here, but I want her right here, right now.

When I fist my cock, she swallows, then licks her lips.

She wants to do this.

Hell *yes*.

I place the back of my hand on her neck to draw her closer to me. I can almost feel her full lips around my cock, her sweet tongue torturing me, when suddenly she freezes. Her pretty, dainty hands on my knees, her eyes come to my wrist.

Fuck.

I didn't realize I'm still wearing my watch. Blinking, she looks from the watch to me in recognition, and her eyes narrow to slits.

"You played me," she hisses. "You fucking played me, and I hate you!" I don't miss the way her voice catches at the end, as if she's about to burst into tears.

She jumps to her feet and runs. There's so much action going on in here, no one notices but me.

She can run.

We'll meet again.

THREE

Cora

I FUCKING HATE HIM. God, I've never hated anyone so much in my life. I want to pound in his beautiful, haughty face.

How stupid am I?

I still have a shift to work at the bar, but when I take my place, my eyes are blurred with angry tears. I blink them away, but Travis notices.

"Hey," he says gently, coming to my side and taking me by the elbow. "You alright?" I swipe my hand angrily across my eyes. I can't take tenderness right now, and he's always so damn sweet.

"I—I'm fine," I blurt out, but he shakes his head.

"Naw," he says in his drawl. "You ain't gonna lie about that. Listen, all the action's in the dungeon tonight. So I can handle this." He gives me a look of concern. "Why don't you take off early?"

I groan.

I can't take off early, because I need the money. "It's okay," I insist, taking a deep breath while I put my apron back on. But Diana is still sitting at the bar and she's taken all of this in.

"Cora. Honey," she says gently. "Don't forget you get ample personal time as part of your job here."

Do I? Or did she just make that up?

I look at her warily. "You don't need to pity me," I say, but it's pleading, not angry. I just want her to understand. I can work hard even when I do lose my shit, *which I never do.*

Except, apparently, when stunningly beautiful men play me for a fool.

Like *that* will ever happen again.

"I'm not. So, go," she says, waving me off. "It's only a few more hours tonight, and Travis is right. It's slow at the bar."

I want out of here so bad, all I need is for them to give me permission, and I'm halfway out the door.

"Thanks, guys," I say, not meeting anyone's eyes. "I owe you."

"Get some rest," Diana says gently. I bite my lip and nod.

"I will," I whisper, not trusting my voice. I'm not used to people being nice to me.

I gather my things and leave. At the door, Brax

looks at me questioningly. "You alright, kiddo?" he asks.

Kiddo again. Do they all see me as a kid? Ugh. *King Douchebag didn't.*

"Yeah, I'm fine," I tell him.

"You sure some asshole didn't give you shit in there?" he asks, raising a brow and cracking his knuckles. I give him a watery grin, my throat suddenly tight. "Just say the word, Cora. I'm happy to kick some ass."

I can't tell him the truth. Brax is like my over-protective big brother, and he'll go pound King Douchebag's head in, which might not be super smart for his job, though I'd personally find it gratifying.

"I'm good. Really," I promise him, then wave good-bye as I head down the street, walking at a really good clip.

And that, right there, thanks to Brax's friendly reminder, is my dilemma. That asshole just infil-trated my workplace, where people who really care about me are. If he keeps showing up... I don't even know what I'll do. It isn't fair. It isn't right. Verge is special to me, and I can't let him ruin that.

So, for tonight, I'll go clear my head. I'm a stupid, stupid girl for letting myself be attracted to that dumbass to begin with and letting him—oh, *God.* The memory heats my cheeks. I'm mad at him for ruining my first taste of kink. I wondered what it would be like to be on the receiving end of pain and pleasure like that... I've fantasized about it now for months. And then my first real taste, and I come apart at the seams.

How was I supposed to know that when I laid over his lap for a spanking it would turn me on *that much?* How was I supposed to know that when he slapped my ass it would feel like a live wire attached directly to my clit, and that my fucking body would respond like that? Hell, he didn't even touch my bare skin to make me come. I was fully *clothed.* Just his hand between my legs... over clothes... was all I needed to hump his hand and climax.

Like a fucking *slut.*

"Grrrrr!" I'm so mad at myself I groan out loud and kick the side of a concrete building. I've marched away from Verge intent on getting to the grocery store so I could grab food and go home, and I haven't paid the slightest bit of attention to where I am.

Shit.

I look around me and my stomach tightens. NYC is not a good place to get lost any time of day, but at night? Not a brilliant idea.

I pull my sweatshirt tighter around my body and hold my bag close, trying to get my bearings. My phone is one the most basic plan there is, but I know I have some GPS thing on it, though I've never used it. I pull it out of my pocket and fumble with it, trying to figure it out, when I finally get the GPS to work. The store I need to get to is about ten minutes from here. I'm not gonna waste money on a cab, and it's nice out, but walking there means walking right through this seedy part of the city.

I need to check on Bailey and Ben, but when I glance at the little battery icon on my phone, it's low. My phone's six years old, which makes it a senior citizen in cell phone years, and the battery life is shot.

But when you're a college student barely making ends meet, new cell phones aren't part of the plan. So I tuck my phone in my pocket, and hope that they call me if they need me.

A loud crowd of guys ahead of me, jostling each other in the street, grows quieter when I near. Without looking their way, I cross to the other side of the street and quicken my pace. I ignore their jeers and catcalls. I don't have far to go now.

I turn the bend fairly running and run smack dab into a couple pressed up against a wall.

"Oh my God, I'm so sorry," I blurt out, but I can tell instantly they're high or drunk, and I just ruined their damn night. The girl's wearing hardly anything, her top pushed up to reveal her silky red bra, crimson lipstick smeared all over his cheek. The guy is big and bulky, wearing leather and jeans, his eyes flashing as he comes my way.

"Sorry?" he says, taking a step toward me. "You bitch. You just walked right into me and my girl. Weren't you watching where you're going?"

The girl giggles and wobbles on her feet like she's about to topple over. He grins at her and grabs me by the arm, glancing her way. He's trying to impress her by manhandling me, and it's working.

"Let me go," I tell him, trying to appear brave though my voice wavers. "My friends are on the NYPD, and if I tell them you assaulted me..."

He snorts. "Like fuck they are."

"I'm not bluffing," I tell him, and I'm not. Zoe and Zack would throw his ass in jail for this.

I scream when he throws me against the wall. My head hits concrete and my phone falls to the ground, shattering. He's advancing on me now, and I can't help but defend myself. I kick him, hitting him right in the shin. Doubling over, he curses, and when he stands he shoves me into the wall. Without warning, he backhands my jaw. Pain blossoms across my mouth and I taste copper. I lift my hands to defend myself; the two of them are no match for just one of me, and the girl is at me now. She grabs me by the hair, and I scream, when the guy reaches into his pocket and flips open a blade.

At the sight, I scream and twist, trying to get away.

"You little bitch. Could've gotten away if you didn't fight back," he says. "You know," he says to the girl. "I think our night just got a lot more interesting."

The girl's got my arms now, pinning them to my side. I'm writhing and squirming but her grip on my hair is immovable. I do the only thing I can. I scream as loudly as I can, trying to shake them.

Will anyone hear me?

I scream again, and again, making myself hoarse, when the blade nicks my collarbone. Searing pain lights my skin on fire, and I twist as far away from him as I can. Dazzling white headlights illuminate the street. He freezes, suspended above me, and my pulse races. The light's blinded me so I can't see a thing. A door slams, and footsteps approach us.

"Let her go." The voice is deep, commanding, and fucking *pissed*.

Immediately, the girl releases me and runs, her hulking boyfriend right behind her. I fall back, panting against the wall, my heart still hammering in my chest. I'm dizzy with fear, and I can't see anything with the blinding light in my eyes.

I freeze when King Douchebag himself rounds the car and comes my way, still dressed in his mime costume from earlier, minus the mask. Though I'm relieved I'm not slashed to bits by the fucking asshole with the knife, it's creepy as fuck that this guy just showed up like a stalker.

"Why?" I ask, bending down to pick up my shattered phone. This has been the worst night of my life, and I want to go home to nurse my wounds. Literally.

"Why me? Are you following me? How did you know I was here?"

"Get in the fucking car," he seethes through gritted teeth.

Charming.

"What?" I say. Even though I could cry with

relief, I'm not really sure that he's a much safer option. "Are you out of your mind?" But no, I already know in my own head that I'm crazy if I think leaving the protection of his car and walking alone where my assailants are likely lying in wait, is a good idea. It's a really dumbass move and I know it. God. This *night*. I want to go home.

I pause and look at him. Actually, I scowl at him. I need a minute to gather my thoughts. Logically, I know he's a member of Verge. My best friends are members there, and I know they're super careful about who they let in. It's clear he's wealthy and powerful, which is *not* a point in his favor, because wealthy, powerful men often get away a hell of a lot more than the average male.

"Cora," he says, and hearing him call my name somehow clears my head. "Get in the fucking car, before I throw you over my shoulder, put you in there, and buckle you in myself."

He's so huge and furious, he just might do it. Jesus, he's beautiful and arrogant, when the street-light catches his blue eyes, sapphires under the glint of moonlight.

"Fucking *now*," he bellows.

"Fine!" I fume. "Fine. But only because I don't want to get my ass kicked, and not because I think you're my knight in shining fucking armor, got it?"

"Whatever," he growls, opening the door.

It's then that I realize he's opening the door to the passenger side of the car, and he has a driver in the driver's seat. Is this like a mini limo or something?

Who is this man? I slide into the back seat, and immediately feel on edge. The sprawling, luxurious interior is bedecked in rich black leather, fragrant and expensive. I'm afraid I'm going to ruin it with my bloody lip, but he's bossed me in here and he can deal with whatever mess since it's his fault.

A second later, he folds himself into the car and slams the door, pushes a button on his watch, and speaks into it like he's fucking Batman.

"Hospital," he says.

"Jesus! I'm not going to the hospital. I don't have time for that," *or money,* I think. "That's such an overreaction. I bumped my head and have a little scrape."

"A little scrape," he growls, pulling a tissue out of his pocket and dabbing at my neck. It stings, so I squirm, but his hand on my shoulder stills me. He's breathing heavily and so am I.

"Stay still," he orders. "You need to doctor that up."

"Fine," I say. "I will when I get home. No hospital."

I avoid his probing eyes and keep my back ramrod straight. I can be stubborn when I need to be, and right now, I need to be.

He lifts his wrist to his mouth again. "Take us on a ride," he orders. "Out of here. Head in the direction of my place."

"I'm not going to your place," I protest. "No *way*. Just take me home."

He glares at me. "I'm not *taking* you to my place," he says. "I said to drive in that direction, because we need to talk about a few things, and I know the drive there will give us time. You won't be getting out of the car there."

Makes total perfect sense. I roll my eyes.

I bite my lip and look away. Now I feel stupid to think he was taking me home, even though that's what he *said*. Why would he do that? He humiliated me. Insulted me. And he's clearly a powerful, wealthy man. What would he want with a poor, messed up girl like me?

"Great," I mutter. "That makes total perfect fucking sense."

"Be quiet," he snaps.

I open my mouth to snap back at him, but he shuts me down with a glare and I'm not sure what I'm going to say anyway. He did just save me.

Jerk.

"I don't want to argue with you right now," he says. "So keep your mouth closed."

"No," I counter, just to be quarrelsome, because who the hell does he think he is?

Narrowed, beautiful eyes meet mine when he responds. "No?"

"That's right, rich guy," I say. "Just because you can throw your money around and buy gilded fucking toilet paper to wipe your arrogant ass, doesn't mean you can cart me around and tell me what to do like you're a fucking god."

"That mouth of yours—"

"You mean the one you wanted wrapped around your cock?"

It gives me a little thrill to see his Adam's apple bob up and down, though he otherwise maintains perfect composure.

"You are so lucky you're not mine, little girl."

"Oh?" I counter. "The age-old threat. Is intimidation really your only play? I'm disappointed."

"I don't give threats, Cora." There's something about the cold, determined way he says this that makes me squirm a little, but I hide it. I don't want him to know that I remember the way it felt to have my wrists pinned helplessly behind my back while his palm spanked against the fullest part of my ass. "And hell yes, I intimidate." He smirks. "And if I recall correctly, you were pretty into the whole intimidation thing earlier."

"Fuck you," I say, oh-so-eloquently.

The dangerous down-turn of his lips is his only reaction. "Do you always mouth off to people who save your ass?" he asks. "How pleasant."

"Save my ass?" I repeat. "More like, stalk my ass. How did you know where I was?"

"I followed you."

I gawk at him in surprise for a minute. "You're not even going to pretend you were doing something normal?"

Shrugging a shoulder, he shakes his head. "I

have nothing to hide. I dommed you. You ran. I followed to make sure you wouldn't do something stupid." Rolling his eyes heavenward, he sighs. "Which, of course, you did."

"You, sir, are an asshole," I say through gritted teeth.

"And you, young lady, are a brat," he counters, crossing his ankle on his knee and shooting me a withering look. "It's no wonder you made your way to Verge. Like somehow, intuitively, you knew how very badly you need to be dommed. How much you crave the release of a scene." His voice lowers, and he takes an accusatory tone. "How badly you need someone to protect you."

I sputter and fume, so angry I can barely form a sentence, but he doesn't stop. "And no, I won't deny that I'm an asshole." Looking away, he yawns. "Makes things easier."

"Impressive."

A silent beat passes and neither of us speaks, but after a moment his voice softens.. "Look at me, please."

I'm still furious at the audacity of this man.

"Do you just tell everyone what to do all the time?"

"Yes."

I don't know what to think of him. Even though he hid who he was tonight, something about him is refreshingly honest, if arrogant. When I look at him, he reaches his hand to me. I flinch when he takes my chin between his fingers and tips my head so the light glints against my upturned face. I want to pry myself away from him, and I hate that I can't, but I'm somehow trapped here. Somehow completely held in his power, though the only touch he has is a gentle one on my chin.

"The asshole split your lip," he growls. To my surprise, he runs his thumb so lightly over the tender spot, it feels almost gentle. "You need to ice that. And put antibiotic cream on this cut." A tender trace of his finger to my neck where the blade nicked me. His voice drops to a reverent, furious whisper. "And I need to track his ass down and make him pay for this."

I swallow, trying to get my nerves together. I can't wrap my brain around what he says and why. The night's overwhelming me with highs and lows, and I blame my confusion on my shaky nerves. No one takes care of me but *me*. And this man can't stand me. Why does he look like he wants to pull me to him and nurse my wounds himself? Why does his voice vibrate with anger when he talks about avenging me?

I finally speak my questions.

"Why?" I whisper.

"Why what?" he whispers back, and for one brief moment I see a glimpse of the man behind the cavalier mask he wears.

"Why do you care?" I need to know.

"Because real men don't hurt women. And anyone who harms someone like you is a fucking coward. I'd like to see him pull that on me."

Hell, I want to see that, too. But I'm not going to fall for his antics, and he's no saint.

"You spanked me," I say, a feeble protest even to my own ears. "And something tells me you'd do more than that if I let you."

To my surprise, his lips quirk up at the edges, but it's so brief I almost miss it. "And I'd do it again," he whispered. "Hell, a part of me thinks it'd do you real good to feel more than my hand on your ass."

"What?" I ask. He's still holding my chin and for some reason, my voice is shaky.

"Take you over my knee," he says, his sapphire gaze molten. "Tie you up. Really take control from you and strip away those layers. To try to tame that wildcat in you." His voice is deep and soft as he runs his thumb over my cheek. "And maybe, just maybe, over time, see some of that anger you wear like a cape fade." He says it almost wistfully.

I can't take this anymore. "Take me home," I whisper. And just like that, the spell is broken. His eyes shutter and I think I've imagined any tenderness.

"Yeah," he says. "Looks like they didn't do much. Ice that damn lip when you get home," he repeats, his voice so distant and cold it feels almost cruel.

I huff in indignation but don't reply.

I can take his anger. I can take his scorn. But I won't let him play with me.

"Your address?" he asks. I don't look at him

when I tell him. I don't want to see whatever the hell is response is—pity? Indignation?

Whatever.

But as soon as we start heading home, I groan.

"What is it?" he snaps. God, this man is irritable.

"I forgot I have to get some groceries," I tell him. Suddenly, I'm tired. So tired I want to curl up in a ball in this ridiculously expensive car of his and fall asleep. "I promised Bailey I'd bring something home."

I lean back against the seat and close my eyes. It's warm and comfortable in here, like laying in a leather armchair.

"Right," he says. "Your boyfriend's waiting."

"Oh, shut up," I tell him. I don't bother to tell him Bailey's my sister. He might have saved me, but he doesn't deserve to know anything about me.

"Watch it, Cora," he warns, in a tone that gets my attention. I blame our earlier scene, for my heartbeat quickening at his admonition. "You're out of free passes. Don't speak to me that way again."

"Or what?" I say, opening my eyes. "You'll spank me again? That's how you do things in Richville?"

Meeting my gaze squarely, his one-word answer makes my pulse race.

"Yes."

I swallow and look away, trying to conjure up indignation. And though he's been a jerk, he's taking me home and just saved me, so I can at least play nice. We ride in silence until his driver pulls up to a small, twenty-four-hour grocery store a block or so away from my apartment.

"Thank you," I tell him, reaching for the handle of the door.

"Oh no, you don't," he says. "You stay here."

He issues orders to his driver, and I watch in surprise as the man enters the store.

"So, wait. You tell everyone what to do and they do it?"

With a bored sigh, he mutters, "Yes. Everyone."

"And if they don't do what you say?"

"I fire them, break up with them, or sue them, depending on who they are."

"Well, then," I mutter. "Must be nice to be king."

"It is."

Another beat passes in silence. I don't know what to say, so I say nothing. Soon, his driver comes out with two huge bags of groceries.

"God," I tell him. "I don't have that much to pay him. I just have—"

He rolls his eyes. "Jesus Christ. Enough."

I clamp my mouth shut, as the man puts the groceries in the back of the car, then comes back to the driver's seat.

"You can't pay for my groceries," I protest. "It's —" But I'm at a loss for words. I truly don't know what to say. My pride aches. I don't like taking handouts. But at the same time, if I can pocket the money I made tonight, it's probably wise.

"I just want it clear that I don't want to be beholden to you," I tell him. "I don't—"

"*Stop.*"

He's quite the conversationalist.

We drive in silence until we pull up in front of my apartment building.

"Call Bailey," he says. "Make him carry the groceries."

I shake my head. "Bailey's asleep," I tell him and decide then I'm done. I'm not going to let him get out of this car thinking I let him get me off even though I have a boyfriend. I'm not that type of girl, and just because he's an asshole doesn't mean he gets to assume *I* am.

"For your information," I tell him. "Bailey's my sister. Not my boyfriend. Maybe going forward it's best if you don't make assumptions about me." I try to toss my head with scorn, but instead just manage to make my hair fall into my face.

"Good night," I tell him, enjoying the look of surprise on his face the split second before he schools his features.

I open the door and step out. His driver carries the groceries and escorts me to the entryway door, then bows his head and bids me good night.

And then he's gone, like he's some sort of angel or demon.

Maybe he's both.

FOUR

Liam

IT'S BEEN a week since I've stepped foot in Club Verge, and it's not because I haven't been thinking about it every damn day. I'm dying to get some relief, to go back to the place where I'm anonymous and respected, but I've had no time. It seems the local damn college is putting up a fuss about my plans for renovations and I'm ready to make heads fucking roll over this.

"Liam, *listen,*" Jake Cronwell, the head lawyer on my staff, leans forward, mopping his bald head with a white handkerchief. "Local college students need an ax to grind. They look for a cause, and those damn millennials are the worst of the lot."

I shake my head while I check my emails and shoot off four replies while Jake drones on and on.

"You're doing nothing illegal. The botanical gardens are beautiful, blah blah blah, but this is prime real estate, and since the owners of The Greenery are in arrears, the time is right."

"I know," I tell him, stifling a yawn. Jake's as dull as hell, and the only reason I keep him on is because he's a damn Pitbull in court.

The phone rings on my desk, so I hit a button to answer it and stop Jake from carrying on.

"Mister Alexander, your dry cleaning has arrived, sir. Shall I bring it into your office?"

"Please," I tell Mandy, my administrative assistant.

A moment later, the door opens, and she steps in, holding my dry cleaning. She's a small, older woman with short white hair, who still wears a dress suit and heels to work every day. She's fairly toppling under the weight of the clothing. I forgot I had my older suit jackets and wool coats cleaned as well. I quickly step away from my desk and relieve her of the burden.

"Oh, Mr. Alexander," she says bashfully. "Always the gentleman."

I think of myself sitting in Club Verge with the feisty little redhead over my knee.

Not always.

"Thank you, Mandy. It's Friday, why don't you take off early?"

"I'd love to, sir. Let me know if there's anything else you need."

I nod, dismissing her. I try to keep my

employees well compensated and happy and have successfully built a team of faithful employees as a result.

I can be ruthless. I can be vicious, even. But they don't need to see that side of me. A man needs a staff he can depend on.

I go back to my desk and check my agenda.

"Got a call from Germany I need to take in five minutes, Jake. You got something else you need to tell me?"

"Sir," he says, a purple vein pulsing in his temple. "You can't dismiss these protestors. They could really have an impact in our plans."

"Since when do I care about some fucking social justice warrior trying to undermine my work?" I ask him with derision. "Like I care. Let them whine. They still live in their parents' basements and don't even pay their own fucking cell phone bills. They can stomp their feet all they want but giving into them is like handing a tantruming toddler candy. Not gonna do it."

God, this shit gets under my collar.

But Jake isn't appeased.

"Liam," he says, leaning forward so his arms brace on the desk in front of me. "I'm not telling you to give them what they want, but we do need to be careful with how we proceed."

I shake my head. "Why?"

With a sigh, he flicks his finger across the screen of his iPad and brings up some footage. "Because of *this*," he says, showing me a picture of a crowd of college students with protest signs standing outside of The Greenery. They're surrounded by reporters from all over the country, but it isn't the reporters that's got my attention.

It's the stunning redhead with her fist in the air, holding a microphone up to a podium.

Leading the fucking protest.

No.

I imagine marching up to that podium and taking her by the arm, then dragging her across my knee right on that fucking stage. I know what that belly feels like against my lap. How satisfying it is to watch the fullest part of her ass take my punishment. The way her mouth parts when I warm her ass... I blink, realizing Jake's continued and I haven't heard a damn word.

"...gotten the attention of the local media," he says. "En masse. And if you don't do some damage control, not only is our project in jeopardy, your reputation is. And you don't need me to tell you, Liam, that matters."

"Of course, it matters," I tell him. He's got a point. They can't stop the actual construction process. We've almost cleared everything legally, and demolition begins in a few weeks. But they can potentially damage my reputation, which seriously does matter. I have a business to run, and Alexander Enterprises does not run its business in a vacuum.

I sigh and pinch the bridge of my nose. "What do you suggest?"

Leaning back in his chair, he can't hide his look of triumph. He's got my attention now, and he knows it.

"A significant charitable donation, perhaps?" he says. "Or maybe reconstruction of a botanical garden on your private property?"

"Why the fuck would I need that? I'm not into Greenery and flowers."

Christ.

"For *publicity*," he insists with a sigh. "Just toss them a bone so they stop crying foul, and we can move on."

I shake my head. "Fine," I say. "I'll think about it."

I don't want to talk about this anymore. I want to track down Cora and punish her for getting involved in this to begin with. "Just make sure our team is sufficiently notified, and that they're ready to play hardball if necessary. Got it?"

Nodding, he gets to his feet. "Got it."

I dismiss him by turning away, and go back to my computer screen, but I can't focus. All I can see is that interfering redhead with that mic in her hand, riling up that crowd.

God, is she ever in need of a firm hand. I let myself fantasize about bringing her here, into my office, and bending her over the enormous mahogany desk. How her little fingerprints would mar the gleaming surface, her cheek flush against the glass top. The little squeal she'd issue when I slammed my palm against her full, gorgeous ass before I took her hard and fast.

I look around my office. It's as big as a suite in one of the most luxurious hotels in Manhattan, with a bathroom and a shower, a small room outfitted with workout equipment, and in the main office area, a huge sofa, small bookshelf, and framed prints of my degrees and accolades.

But beyond this office, the other rooms are vacant. It's Friday night and everyone's gone home but me. I often stay late. Hell, there's a reason why I have suits that stay in my office, workout equipment, a shower, and a pullout sofa.

It's Friday, though. And I have someone to go see.

Pushing a button on my desk, I ring my driver.

"Sir?"

"Ten minutes," I tell him.

"Yes, sir."

I hang up the phone and bring up the footage Jake showed me.

I stare at her mesmerizing eyes, so full of life and fire. Her wild, crazy, vibrant hair. The pert nose dotted in fetching freckles, and full, beautiful lips.

Shutting off my computer, I tidy the area and grab my jacket, before I shut and lock my office.

"Where to, sir? Home?" my driver, Manuel, asks.

I glance at the time. If she's leaving the bookstore in a bit, I just might catch her. What I'll do with her if I do, I have no idea. I can't decide if I want to kiss her pretty, belligerent little lips, or teach her a lesson. None of that little slap and tickle I gave her the other day, but a really good session that makes her cry.

"Books and Cups," I tell him. "I need to check something."

"Right away, sir." It takes us only a few minutes to get there.

I don't have a plan. I have no idea what I'm going to say to her. Maybe I'm just checking on her. Like a fucking altruist. Because that's what Liam Alexander is, a philanthropist.

Christ.

Walking into the store, I only see the owner behind the desk. She waves and smiles at me, then turns to serve a customer. I feel a little disappointed. No, I feel a lot disappointed. I came in here ready to fight, and she isn't here.

I'll have to ask around.

Taking a book off a shelf, I fan thoughtlessly through the pages when I hear a familiar voice. My heartbeat accelerates like a damn teen's.

"Feminism through the Ages? Really?"

She's standing a few feet apart from me, with her hands on her hips.

"Yes," I tell her in a bored voice. "I like to see what stupidity they're propagating now."

The comment has the desired effect, as her fetching cheeks flush pink. "I—you—how *dare* you!" she fumes.

"How dare I what?" I ask. "Critique a cause that's near and dear to you?"

"I—*argggh,*" I've rendered her speechless.

Enough of this. I close the book and place it back on the shelf, rounding on her.

"How dare *you?*" I ask. I step toward her and she backpedals, her pretty eyes widening. "Getting involved in things that don't involve you. Sticking your nose where it doesn't belong."

Blinking, she pauses, then looks wildly about the store as if she's going to call for help. Hell, I'm waiting for it.

But she doesn't.

"What are you talking about?" she says. "I have no idea—oh. Oh, no. Oh, God!"

Her sudden change of tone surprises me.

"What?" I scowl at her.

Closing her eyes, she smacks her forehead. "I'm sorry," she says. "We'll have to resume our argument later. I have to go."

"Go? Where?"

Glancing at the clock on the wall, she shakes her head, and to my surprise, her eyes fill with tears. "You don't care, so why should I tell you?" she says. "I forgot something." Her voice catches at the end, and for some reason, something unfamiliar claws at my chest. I fight the urge to draw her to me and hold her. "Something super important."

"Our conversation is important," I counter.

"Something *more* important," she says, her eyes flashing at me.

Good girl.

The thought comes unbidden when she challenges me.

I wonder what she'd do to me if she pleased me.

I love the pretty way her eyes glow when she's mad.

You're so pretty when you're angry.

"I see. And now you're late?"

"Yes," she whispers.

"You know, they make these things called calendars," I tell her with a frown. She really should get her act together. "And smartphones with reminders."

"Do they?" she asks, her head tipped to the side. "And they also make these things called *douches*. Do you know what they are? They're used to—"

But the door to the bookstore opens and she clamps her mouth shut.

This time, I do speak it out loud. Taking a step closer to her, I whisper, "Good girl. You really do not want to complete that sentence, do you, Cora?" Leaning in, I let my thumb brush her delicate collarbone, when I whisper, "Or did you forget? What it felt like to be strewn over my lap, helpless, while I spanked you?"

"Oh God," she whispers, shaking her head, but I can feel her trembling. "Please."

"Please, what? Make you come again?" I shake my head and tsk like I'm scolding an errant child.

"No, sweetheart. Not unless you beg. And only good girls get rewards."

Huffing out a breath, she turns from me, but I can see it takes some effort. "I have to go," she whispers. I almost regret being a jerk.

"Tell me," I order.

"No, I—"

"Now," I insist in my sternest tone. Christ, the woman would do well with a folded belt across her ass.

People call me convincing. Persuasive.

I get what I want.

"Parent-teacher night," she says, not meeting my eyes. "I promised Bailey I would be there, and it's just starting. By the time I can get a ride..."

I'm not thinking straight. I should let her go. I should walk away. Hell, I shouldn't even be here.

I've let my impulses run crazy, like wild stallions, and I'm losing self-control. Losing? Hell, I've already lost it.

"I have a driver," I tell her. "He'll take you. Let's go."

"What?" she sputters. "I can't—"

I give her an angry glare. "Why not? You've been in my car before. And you're already late."

Worrying her lip, she glances around the store. I can see when she finally makes the decision, for the wrinkles on her forehead soften, and she casts her eyes down.

"Yes, please."

"Go tell your boss," I say. "But we need to go now if we're going to get there on time."

She wastes no time in running to the front of the store. After a quick conversation with Marla, who looks my way warily but nods, she grabs her bag and runs to me.

"Thank you," she says. "I'm... thank you," she repeats.

"You're welcome," I tell her.

"Is this a truce?" she asks.

Damn, she's cute. "Yeah," I say with a smirk. "Cease fire."

For the first time since I've met her, she smiles, and hell if it isn't gorgeous.

I lead her to where my car waits and flick the button so the screen comes down between the back and front cab.

"Where to, sir?"

I jerk my head at her. "Wherever she needs to go."

When she gives him the name of the closest high school, I blink in surprise.

Why a high school? Cora has some explaining to do.

I don't know why I want to know these things. I don't know why I have to ask her. But I like to know exactly what hand I'm playing.

Flicking the button to make the divider go back up again, I turn to her.

"So, you're going to parent-teacher night. Why?"

Cora sits awkwardly, twisting her hands in her lap, but she meets my eyes without blinking.

"My mom was an alcoholic who died about six months ago in prison. She and my dad didn't grow up around here, but she relocated after my dad was killed overseas."

"Overseas?"

"He was in the military," she explains. "Naval officer. After losing him, my mom... made some very bad choices."

"I see."

"So, I fought for, and won, custody of Bailey and Ben."

I know who Bailey is. "Ben?"

"My brother."

Shit. She's the guardian of two children, she's a college student, and holds down two jobs?

I could change her life without blinking an eye. *No.*

I don't give to charity causes like hers. I give to places that will benefit my career. I don't believe in handouts. And I *don't* get involved with women saddled with children.

Why am I letting her get to me?

"So that's it."

"And you work at Verge because..."

Leaning forward, she lowers her voice. "I work at Verge because I like the people there. I... have never scened with anyone, and I don't plan to. I don't even want to."

Oh, but the way her cheeks pink tell another story.

I nod but can't help smirking a little. I try to hide it, but she notices.

"Don't laugh at me," she says through gritted teeth. "*Please*. That was a... momentary lapse in judgment, and I regret it."

I don't respond at first, just tap my knee. Suggesting. When her eyes travel to my hand on my knee, she flushes a deeper shade of pink and looks away. God, I'm an asshole, but I can't help teasing her.

"I... I don't want to make a mistake that could cost me custody," she blurts out. "*Ever*."

"Bailey's how old again?" I ask.

"Fourteen," she says. "Not long and she'll be an adult herself."

"And Ben?"

"Ten."

I inhale deeply and let the breath out slowly, drumming my fingers on my lap while I look out the window, before I turn to her. "That's a lot on your plate, Cora."

Let me take some of that off for you.

No. No way.

"It is, but I do fine," she says.

"Do you?" I wonder. Reaching for her chin, I turn her gaze to mine. I like the soft feel of her skin beneath my fingers. The way she looks at me with slightly parted lips, unaccustomed to the tender gesture. "When was the last time you ate a decent meal, Cora?"

Swallowing, she tries to look away, but a sharp pull on her chin keeps her gaze locked on mine.

"I don't need to eat much," she says. "I'm too chubby as it is."

A growl rises in my chest. "Don't you ever fucking say a thing like that to me again. If you were mine, I'd turn you over my knee for a comment like that."

With her chin held vulnerable in my grasp, the way she swallows is clear. "I'm not yours," she whispers.

Not yet.

"Answer the question."

Sighing, she finally whispers. "It's been a very long time. But I get by."

I'll feed her tonight, then let her go.

As soon as the thought crosses my mind, I release her chin. She's not a stray dog I found on the street who can eat my table scraps and scamper into the night.

Christ.

Why do I want the one thing I can't have?

We pull up to the school and I wave my hand. "Go," I tell her. "Be as quick as you can. I'm assuming you have a shift at Verge tonight?"

"Yes."

"Then make it quick if we're getting food before you go."

But she doesn't move. She stares at me until I snap my fingers and point to the door.

"Don't try me, woman." I'm out of patience, but what she doesn't know is that I'm mad at myself, not her.

Without another word, she's gone.

When the door shuts, I groan.

What the fuck am I doing?

FIVE

Cora

I SHOULD NOT BE TAKING handouts from him.

I should not.

But how can I let my pride get in the way of keeping me from what I really need? I screwed up tonight. I promised Bailey I would go and meet every one of her teachers.

I tell myself to stop thinking about the fact that he's waiting for me.

To stop thinking about the fact that after I'm finished here, he's buying me dinner. My stomach aches with hunger. I've had nothing but a bowl of oatmeal since eight o'clock this morning, and it was plain, so it didn't even taste good.

I need to *stop thinking* how he made my pulse

race with just the reminder of how he took me over his lap.

God. I'm getting in too deep, and I don't even know his name.

All eyes are on me as I step out of his massive black car that looks like it belongs in the rich part of town, instead of the high school.

"Well, well, well," someone mutters, but when I turn to see who it is, they're already gone.

I'm half angry at myself for letting him take me, and half shocked at my luck. What did I do to deserve a man like him taking care of me?

But the better question is... what will he expect in return?

I go to get my phone out of my bag when I remember my phone is broken, and I haven't had the time or money to replace it since that night a week ago.

Has it been so long?

Instead, I take the crumpled piece of paper out of my pocket with Bailey's schedule on it, and glance at the time on the huge round clock on the wall. It wasn't so long ago I went to this very school myself, and I know this place like the back of my hand.

I go to her first class, and though the young English teacher looks surprised when she sees me, she has nothing but good things to say about Bailey. The second class goes much the same as the first, but when I get to the third, freshman Biology, I find the door locked. I stand back and look at the number on the door.

Yep. I'm at the right place. Then why is no one here? I look up and down the crowded hall, when I finally see a tall, lanky guy with a tweed jacket and glasses perched on his nose approach me.

Something in me grows sad. I've never asked Bailey anything about her teachers. I don't know what they look like, who's nice, what they wear or how they treat her. I glance at her grades, but they're good, and I've never done anything beyond that.

Her whole life has changed, and I don't even realize until her teacher opens the classroom door, that I've failed her. Like I fail everyone. Marla tonight, because I had to bail on my shift. Ben, because he's been asking me to play a game of chess for a damn month.

I have no time. How can I do everything that I'm supposed to?

I blame the hunger for making my eyes water. This is so stupid. I shake my head and enter the classroom.

"Hi," I say brightly, extending my hand. The teacher takes it and shakes.

"Hi," he says. "You do know this is parent-teacher night, right? Students aren't supposed to be here."

My traitorous pale cheeks flame. "I'm—I'm guardian to Bailey Myers," I tell him.

Frowning, he pulls out a paper on his desk and looks at it. "I see. Forgive me, Ms..."

"Cora Myers," I supply.

"Forgive me, Ms. Myers, but you look a bit young to be guardian to a young woman in high school."

"Of course," I say, my temperature rising. "I have custody of Bailey after the death of my mother. And I came here tonight to touch base with each of her teachers. Do you have any concerns?"

I want to leave. I hate how little he makes me feel, like I'm barely old enough to know my ABC's, much less raise a teenager.

And hell, if he isn't right.

We talk about Bailey and her grades, but before I leave, he apparently thinks it's his duty to give me a little advice.

Lucky me.

"I admire your courage, Ms. Myers," he tells me. "It's difficult at your age to make the right decisions."

"It's difficult at any age to make the right decisions," I reply. I hate when people look down on me because of my age. My mother made shit decisions, and she was a lot older than I am. Gathering up my papers and bag with a smile plastered to my face, I get up to leave. It's none of his damn business.

"Certainly," he says with a nod. "Just be sure you don't make a decision that will jeopardize what matters to you."

Who the hell is he?

I finally leave his class and look in chagrin at my sheet. There are two more classes I need to visit, and he's waiting for me. In his private car. What sort of bizarre situation is this?

I don't even know his name.

God. How can I not even know his name? I need to find out who he is.

For a minute, I contemplate running. Going out the back door and catching a cab to Verge and leaving Mr. High and Mighty to his own devices. But then I think better of it. I don't need to make any enemies.

I go through the motions for the next classes and wish I didn't have to work tonight. I want to go home and see Bailey and Ben. Play that game of chess with Ben and talk to Bailey about meeting all her teachers, which one's funny, which one's grumpy, and how her math teacher is really kinda cute. But I can't. I have to work again, and God if that doesn't burn.

So, by the time I go outside, I half expect the stranger to be gone, but he isn't. The black car still waits for me. I feel a bit like Cinderella making my way toward him. Any minute, the clock will strike midnight, and the car turn into an enchanted pumpkin.

I'm lightheaded with hunger, and tired. I've done so much today already, I'm exhausted.

Food will be good. I just have to play nice for a little while. I can't let my mouth ruin everything, like I usually do.

When I reach the car, I tap on the window awkwardly. What else am I supposed to do? I blink to myself when Manuel comes to my side of the car, bows, and opens the door for me.

"Thank you," I murmur, before I slide myself into the car.

"Took a while," he mutters, glancing at that god-awful Rolex.

"Well, she's taking six classes," I say. "And the school's big. You didn't have to wait."

He frowns and issues a command to the driver.

"Where are you taking me?" I ask him. "And... um... one more question."

Turning to face me with those vibrant blue eyes locked on mine, he quirks a lip up at me. "Yeah?"

"What's your name?"

To my surprise, he doesn't answer at first. Stroking his chin contemplatively, he shakes his head.

"Most women call me sir."

I literally guffaw. "I, *sir*, do not." I snort with derision.

"You just did," he says, and the man actually *smiles*. My heart does a crazy little patter in my chest at the sight of him smiling. Honest to God, I thought he was gorgeous when he scowled. When he smiles...

"You didn't answer the question," I prod.

"We're getting pizza," he says. "Next time, I'll give you fair warning so you can put on something a little more appropriate, and I'll take you to a nicer place."

"I love pizza," I blurt out. "It's like my favorite thing." I can't stop my mouth, and I say one stupid thing after another.

"Yeah? Have you ever eaten it on a rooftop?"

"Hell *no,* I haven't. Shut *up!* Are you kidding me?" I smack his chest, but he pinches my wrist between his fingers and glides it down the silky suit jacket.

"No hitting, little girl," he says, the humor fading, and in its place, a dangerous, predatory look lurks in his eyes. My sudden attempt at being light-hearted fades.

Little girl does funny things to my chest. I like that he makes me feel little. Hearing him say it? I like that even more.

"And no, I'm not kidding," he says. "There's a place near Verge that serves rooftop pizza cooked in brick ovens."

"Wait, wait. Is this a date?"

A smile ghosts his lips again. "No. If it were a date, I'd have to kiss you."

Flushing a bit, I shrug a shoulder. "You say it as if it were a chore."

The heat in the inside of the car is suddenly sweltering. God, what is wrong with me? I'm flirting with him and this guy's a jerk. He's bossy and rich and arrogant as fuck, and I'm joking about —I don't know—I have no idea what I'm...

Because he's running his fingers through my

hair, gentle pressure on the back of my head pulling me closer to him. He smells so good, the way I'd imagine the men on the cover of glossy magazines to smell, a gentle yet seductive masculine scent that makes me feel all feminine and pretty. I don't know what to do with my hands, they're awkward and clumsy, but soon I forget everything.

Everything but his lips on mine.

The electricity between the two of us hums like mad, as if our pulses are fused together. I'm soft, so soft, malleable and silky when I'm in his arms like this. I've kissed boys before, but I've never been kissed like this.

Kissed by a man who wants me.

Kissed by a man who takes what he wants.

I don't even know how it happens, but I'm flat on my back on my seat, my wrists captured in his strong fingers, gentle but firm like silken cuffs. I'm moaning, sinking, under his spell. I've lost all control.

I like that.

When he pulls away his eyes are electric, and he's panting slightly.

"Jesus Christ," he whispers.

I'm affecting him, too, and the knowledge is a mini victory.

"Your name," I whisper back.

"If I tell you my name, you promise me you won't run," he says. His tone grows harsh. "*Promise.*"

An order.

I swallow, my pulse suddenly racing.

"Do it," I whisper. "I promise."

A beat passes before he speaks again. "My name is Liam Alexander."

I close my eyes and groan.

SIX

Liam

I WANT her and I hate that I do.

I fucking want her, and I shouldn't.

She's a damn brat, and way too young for me. Poorer than a church mouse and worst of all? She's got *kids* she's responsible for. Almost as bad as a single mom and *that* is fucking anathema to me. I don't care who a woman is, how beautiful she is, how much I enjoy her... children are a hard limit.

A *hard fucking limit*.

Why am I even thinking about what I want to propose?

The elite women I socialize with don't pose a challenge to me. The only challenge is who to pick. Cora, though... Cora is playing hard to get, and I doubt it's even intentional.

After I told her my name, she closed her eyes and groaned, and I got my shit together. I released her and smoothed out my suit while she righted her hair and grumbled, though I didn't miss the flush on her cheeks and chest, the wide, bright eyes and the way her pretty lips are slightly parted.

Christ, what I'd do with that mouth.

"You look oh so happy to be going out to eat with me," she mutters, shaking her head and staring out the window. "Not super sure what your problem is."

My problem is her, damn it.

I don't do relationships with strings attached. Hell, the past half dozen relationships I had, we had contracts. There wasn't anything beyond the bedroom involved. The exchange of power. Control.

I like what I want, and what I want is a woman who obeys me, who accompanies me to events, and who leaves with a cool sum of cash so there are no hard feelings when I'm ready to move on.

This is not good.

Not to mention the fact that she's openly protesting the largest business deal I've had in well over a decade.

Christ, I'm a moron.

Everything in me says, *run,* and yet here I am, bringing her to the rooftop of *Fiamatta* because the girl needs a good fucking meal, and I love this place. It's casual enough for what she's wearing, and the rooftop gives us privacy because I already called in and reserved it.

"You're the guy," she says, her lips thinning when she pauses between words. *"You're* the guy that wants to pave The Greenery."

I shrug. "You make it sound like I want to skin live rabbits and sell their fur. I'm not *that* cruel, Ms. Myers. I'm a businessman. And I prefer not to discuss that at the moment."

"No? You don't make sense, though. You don't know me at all and clearly don't even like me. And yet here I am, in the back of your fancy-pants car, getting something to eat. I don't know what it is you want from me."

She will.

God, that mouth of hers.

It's been too long since I've had a contract with a woman, and I haven't had one with a kink virgin like her. What I could introduce her to. What I could show her...

"Tonight, I want dinner," I tell her. "Now stop complaining for a damn minute, will you? Are you hungry or not?

"Starving," she says, glaring.

I roll my eyes and huff out a breath. After one good night with her hands cuffed behind her back while sucking my cock, a jeweled plug in her ass, and her body striped good and well with a short-handled whip, I bet she'd find that mouth of hers doesn't run so freely.

My cock hardens. God, do I want a chance to

tame this wild girl. If only she didn't get on my nerves so much.

"Then for the love of God, shut up and let's get something to eat."

"How charming. You tell all your dates to shut up?"

"No," I mutter between clenched teeth. I give her a pointed look. "I typically gag them if they're mouthy, after I give them a good spanking."

It's actually amusing how she opens her mouth then clamps it shut, her bright eyes wide.

"I—you—"

But we've pulled up to the curb and Manuel is opening the door. "They're waiting for you, sir. Go right on up."

We get out of the car, but before we enter the restaurant, I take her hand.

"A quick word with you before we go upstairs," I tell her.

Pretty, angry eyes meet mine. "Yes, *sir?*" she parrots.

"Behave yourself. My reputation matters to me. I don't allow people to speak to me the way you have, and if you do, I'll put an end to it.'

Rolling her eyes, she asks, "Oh? What will you do, daddy? Spank me?" Oh, that lyrical little voice of hers wouldn't sound so saucy if she was panting out a plea.

"Not yet," I murmur. "A spanking on bare skin is far more effective, but I don't like the idea of anyone else's eyes on you but me. Sorry to disappoint you, but that will have to wait."

I like the way her pretty mouth falls open when I continue. That one little spanking over her fully-clothed ass was just a warning.

"If you get mouthy, I'll kiss you again to silence that tongue of yours. Got it?"

"Sounds terrible," she mutters.

"Cora," I warn.

"Silencing me with a kiss. Next thing you know, you'll punish me with chocolate cake."

I sigh with practiced patience.

"Buy me roses to teach me a lesson?"

Christ, she's mouthy. I shake my head, take her wrist, and give her a sharp crack to the ass when we approach the entryway door. The spank has the desired effect and she clamps her mouth shut.

We'll see how much she runs her mouth when I make her the offer.

"Enough. Let's get something to eat. We have a few things to discuss."

When the uniformed waiter opens the door and bows to us, the smell of fresh-baked bread, roasted garlic, and basil wafts through the air. I notice Cora swallow hard, her mouth closed.

Why is she starving? Does she not have enough money for food? Does she get too distracted with her work that she doesn't take the time to care for herself? Does she have some kind of preposterous notion in her mind that she doesn't fit the ideal body type and needs to starve herself to lose weight?

I want to find out.

There are so many things about her I want to know, and I hate that I do. It's dangerous. I prefer being aloof to women like her.

I walk in silence ahead of her and she follows, until we've reached the secluded round table on the rooftop. It's a pleasantly warm fall evening, and a gentle breeze kicks up. The tables are laden with white fabric tablecloths and little bud vases with single stems of white roses. Pleasant strings of classical music plays in the background. I normally dine here alone, and this is the first time I've brought a guest.

"Well isn't this place fancy," she says, but I can't tell if her tone is derisive or teasing.

"It's fine," I mutter, pulling out her chair for her.

"Why'd you do that?" she asks.

"Do what?"

"Pull out the chair for me."

Is she serious?

"Because I'm a gentleman," I tell her. "Now sit your ass down."

With a snort, she plunks herself down and I adjust her at the table.

"Gentleman my ass," she mutters. "I don't know if a gentleman would tell me to sit my ass down."

"You'd try the patience of a saint," I tell her,

taking my own seat across from her and signaling the waiter to bring us the wine menu.

"And what would I do to a sinner?" Her eyes are bright but dancing, I only catch them for a second before she casts her gaze away and eyes a roll from the basket on the table. She doesn't touch it.

"Time will tell."

That brings the faint flush to her cheeks that I love. Reaching for a roll myself, I butter it and we sit in comfortable silence. She still eats nothing.

"No food menu," she says.

"We don't need one," I tell her. "I know exactly what to order."

"Is that right?" she asks. Leaning across the table, she lowers her voice. "You don't know me at all. How would you know what I like?"

And suddenly, I'm not sure we're talking about dinner.

I lean closer to her, take a bread roll from the basket, and rip it open. Steam wafts in the air between us, while I slather some butter on the roll. I hand it to her.

"Because you're predictable," I tell her. "And reading you is like reading a first-grade primer."

It astonishes me how quickly those eyes go from curious to angry in a split second.

"I'm not a primer," she chokes out.

"Didn't say you were."

"You did!"

"Did not."

"You just said—"

"I said you were easy to read, not that you *were* the primer. Oh, no. Not at all, Cora. You're far more complex than that."

She takes a savage bite out of the roll while glaring at me.

"Keep scowling at me like that, your face could get stuck that way," I tell her, remembering the old adage my grandma taught me.

"Oh?" she says. "Tell me why I'm so easy to read. What am I saying with my body language or whatever?"

The waiter comes to our table, so I order a bottle of wine for us both. The waiter pours us each a glass, and when we're finally alone, I give her my answer.

"It's partly in your body language," I tell her. "You're overwhelmed and busy, and while other people you go to school with are stressing over midterms and exams, and what to wear, you're worried about paying your bills. Making sure your brother and sister get what they need. Keeping your grades high while you juggle the responsibilities a woman your age shouldn't have to bear."

She's stopped chewing, but the side of her cheek bulges out, like she's got half a loaf in there she forgot what to do with.

Finally, she swallows. "Well, that's obvious," she says. "Any college student who was guardian to their siblings would feel the same."

"Maybe," I allow. "But that isn't all I'm reading from you."

She lifts her wine and drains half the glass in one large gulp,

I barely stifle a smile. I'm getting to her.

"What else is there?" she says with a shoulder shrug.

I take a slow drink from my wine glass while I carefully formulate my reply.

"The other night at Verge," I tell her. "You were looking for something or someone. Something to keep your mind off whatever it is that troubles you. Someone who would be willing to do that for you."

"I was not," she says, finishing her glass of wine.

"Don't lie to yourself, sweetheart," I tell her. "And don't lie to *me*. You're a bartender at the most well-respected kink club in the state. And you didn't want to know what it was like to submit?"

"I—it was more curiosity than anything," she says. "But laying over your lap for a spanking is hardly the same as looking for someone to relieve me of my responsibilities."

I shake my head. "You can deny what's written right across your face, Cora," I tell her. "You want someone to take care of you. Protect you. Someone you can rely on."

This time, she doesn't respond at first, but sits immobile at the table. She doesn't touch the bread or wine, but just sits. Contemplating?

Our pizza arrives, and our waiter slides a piece on each of our plates.

"Eat," I tell her. "We've got to get to the club."

In silence, she eats her food, and I can tell she likes it by the way she licks her lips and her gaze softens.

"I don't like that you think I'm so predictable," she says. "It makes me feel stupid and shallow."

"And that's exactly the type of thing I wouldn't allow if you were mine."

Blinking, she looks genuinely confused. "What?"

"The self-deprecation."

Shaking her head, she takes a second slice of pizza.

"And to be clear, I don't think you're predictable. There are a handful of things about you I've surmised, but there are many things I have not." It's time to change the subject. "Tell me about your family."

"You first."

"Alright." I take a sip of wine and lean back in my chair. "My parents are socialites, the elite. They're retired and remote, and I like it that way. My father is an asshole with no low he wouldn't stoop to to get ahead. And he did. Over and over again. My mom was happy as long as she got what she wanted, which, in her case, was diamonds and furs and servants to wait on her. She wanted nothing to do with me, and less to do with my father."

Cora's eyes widen. "Wow."

I shrug. "Yeah. So, they're retired and hate each other, and I only have to see them on holidays."

"Sounds... lovely," she murmurs. "So... no siblings. No fond childhood memories..."

"Right. I don't want to talk about my parents. There's no love lost on either account."

"That's so sad," she murmurs.

"So your mom was an alcoholic who died in jail," I say. "Your father died overseas in the military, and now you have custody of two children."

"Right."

"How do you do it?"

"Do what?" she asks.

"Hold down two jobs, go to college, and parent two kids?"

I watch her cast her gaze away from mine when she eats her pizza. Swallowing, she finally answers. "I don't do it well, as evidenced by my mad scramble to get to parent-teacher night tonight. I see Ben and Bailey on the weekends, but it isn't nearly enough time. My grades are good, but only because I've been miraculously gifted the ability to do well academically without much effort. I just retain information easily."

Shrugging, she looks back at me. "Now let's get to the real reason why we're here, Mr. Alexander."

God, her spunk. No pussy footing around the real issues with this one.

"The real reason? You were hungry and so was

I. I wanted to talk to you in private, so I brought you here."

With her eyes on mine, she sips more wine, bringing a color to her cheeks that makes her fetching.

"You take poor college girls for uber expensive rooftop pizza on a whim often?" she asks.

This wasn't how I would propose things to her. Not now. Not like this. But she's asking, so I'll give her the bald truth.

"I'm a man with particular tastes, Cora," I tell her.

She snorts.

God, she needs her ass whipped.

"Aren't we all?" she murmurs, before taking another bite of her pizza.

"Perhaps. But I don't do relationships. I ask for a simple agreement. Eight weeks where you follow my rules."

"Wait. *What?*"

"I'm offering you a proposition."

I shouldn't do this. I *should not* do this.

But I can't fucking help it. I want her.

"Is that so?" she asks, her eyes wide with shock. "And what might that be?"

"For two months, you'll agree to be my submissive. During that time, I ask that you step down as bartender of Verge, though you may keep your job at the bookstore."

"*What?*"

"I will expect you to accompany me on dates

and scene regularly with me at Club Verge. In turn, I will see to your utmost needs, and pay you amply."

"You're insane," she mutters.

I write down a number on a napkin and show it to her, enjoying how she stills in shock.

"What's that?" she whispers.

"The payment I'll give you for following my terms."

Her eyes widen and she bites her lip, brows furrowed. I watch how she wrestles with her needs and reservations, not knowing how to respond. Does the idea intrigue her?

"I can't do this," she finally whispers. "I can't... no." She's on her feet. With eyes flashing at me, she's backing away. "And you're an asshole for even offering. You knew I was poor. You knew how hard it would be to say no. And still, you had the audacity to taunt me like this. *No*. You think everyone has the inclination to obey you, just because you're wealthy and powerful? There are some things, Mr. Alexander, that *money* simply can't buy."

I watch her leave and pull up my phone to instruct Manuel to take her to wherever she needs to go. She can take off but she'll do it safely.

I smile to myself as I watch her go.

This was the first conversation we've had about my proposal. It won't be the last.

SEVEN

Cora

THE GUY HAS SUCH NERVE. I can't believe he wanted me to sign my life away to him like that, like I'm some sort of sex slave. Is he for real? Incredible.

I go outside, only to find Manuel waiting for me. "Mister Alexander says to take you wherever you need to go."

"I'm fine on my own," I say, not wanting to take another handout from this guy. But I have no idea where exactly in the city we are, I have to get home and check on Bailey and Ben before my shift starts, and a taxi is an expense I can't afford.

"Miss, please," the driver says. "It's no trouble. And Mr. Alexander doesn't take no for an answer."

"Well sometimes it's illegal insisting someone

won't take no for an answer!" I snap. But he remains unruffled.

"In this case, it's totally legal," he says placidly. "Now, please get in the car."

"Fine," I huff. "Just take me home."

God, maybe I need to call in sick. What if he goes to Verge? Damn it. I don't want him and his fucking proposal. He can shove it up his ass.

The city whips by as he takes me home.

"So, you're going to go back and get him?" I ask. "He's just going to sit on the roof alone eating million-dollar pizza until you come back?"

Manuel's lips twitch. "If he chooses. Or, he can call another driver. He's messaged me and told me to wait for you, so he'll likely do that."

"Maybe he should just hire a private jet," I mutter.

Manuel shrugs. "He has. The inner city is a bit impractical for the jet, though."

God!

We pull up outside my apartment building, and I'm immediately struck with how incongruous it is to have this fancy, gleaming car in the midst of such a low-income area. We live in the poorest section of the city, a high-rise with apartments with way too many people crammed into it. When I step out of the car, a baby wails in the distance, and someone's playing loud, raucous music. A billow of cigarette smoke wafts in my direction. I sputter and turn to Manuel, who steps out of the vehicle and takes his place by my side like he's my personal bodyguard.

To be honest, I could get used to this.

I ignore the whispers and catcalls.

"Listen," I tell him. "I can take it from there."

"Mr. Alexander gave me orders, ma'am. Escort you to your residence, then wait until you need another ride."

"So, you have to babysit me?" I ask, hating that I'm secretly pleased by the gesture. "Like I'm a child?"

He quirks a brow. "You might do well with a nap."

Now I know why he hired *this* guy.

I sigh and let him walk me to my apartment.

"I'll be waiting down here," he says, then salutes me before he leaves.

I let myself in, step over a couple that's doing something grossly sexual on the floor of our entry-way, pass two teens discreetly vaping under the stairwell, and take the stairs two at a time until I get to our apartment.

I'm glad Liam didn't come. I'd hate for him to have to see this.

Why do I care?

Opening the door to our apartment, I step in and shut the door quickly. Ben drops the book he's reading and dives toward me, hugging me around the middle so hard I lose my breath. Bailey waves a wooden spoon to me from the kitchen and smiles at Ben's antics.

"You actually came home for dinner?" Ben

asks, and I feel a little guilty. The designer pizza weighs heavily in my stomach.

"Well, to be honest, I just came home to see you two," I tell him. "I ate dinner with a friend already."

Friend?

More like FRENEMY.

Liam Frenemy Alexander.

"What'd you eat?" Bailey asks.

"Pizza." I don't need to tell them it was million-dollar pizza on a rooftop.

"Ha! That's what we're having." She opens the stove and takes a pizza out of the oven. "It's one of the ones you got the other night."

"Oh, right," I tell her with a sad attempt at a laugh. Why do I feel so guilty? Why do I have to hide Liam from them? *Because you don't want them to know how badly you are at taking care of them*, a nasty little voice whispers through me.

I sit at the dining room table while they eat and talk about school and how things are going.

"So... how was parent-teacher night?" Bailey asks, not meeting my eyes. She's dying to know but trying to play it safe.

"Oh, it went well." I tell her. "Everyone says you're doing great in school. I was a little late but still managed to see everyone."

She beams at me before she takes another bite of pizza.

"I'm glad you two are good students. Honest to God, I don't know how I'd do it otherwise."

"Wellll," Ben says. He's ten-years-old with the

same flaming red hair that I have, his face a mass of freckles. Biting his lip, he looks away. "Can't really tell you I did super great on my spelling quiz."

"Oh?" I ask pointedly. "Why not?"

"Well, the words were stupid," he says, his eyes flashing. "They all had *silent letters*. Which is dumb. D-u-m. Who needs that "b"? It's just plain *dumb*." He snickers.

"You know you get in trouble if your grades sink, Ben. You've got to do your best."

"I know," he says. "Well I get to take it again tomorrow."

"Okay, good." I'm hard on them about their grades, because it's all they've got left. The only way I'm even able to go to college is because I got a scholarship. There's no way we'd be able to afford anything else and I'm depending on their grades to get them scholarships too.

We talk easily, until Bailey gives me a coy look. "So," she says. "Jennifer's mom told Andrea's mom who told Andrea who told me, that you got into a fancy-pants car at school."

I *knew* someone would see.

"Mhm," I say, not meeting her eyes, and pretending to be very interested in the permission form I have to sign for Ben's science class.

"Mhm?" she parrots. "What's that supposed to mean? Did you, or didn't you?"

I give her a withering look. She looks just like me, except her eyes are a shade darker and she's much thinner, like the lithe limbs of a willow tree.

"I did. And that's all I'm telling you."

"Really? OMG, Cora, come *on.* You haven't had a boyfriend in like years, and the first time you go on a date with some guy, you don't even tell us?"

I hold up my hand in protest. "There's no *date.* He's just a guy I know."

"So, he didn't buy you food?"

"Well, he did, but—"

"Did he flirt?"

"I, well I don't *exactly* know if—"

"Did he kiss you!?"

I sigh but don't respond. Bailey's a romantic matchmaker who loves to be involved in every single romantic relationship she can.

"Enough, Bailey. Change the subject *now.*"

Deflated, she leans back in her chair and shreds her pizza with her fingers into little squares she pops in her mouth.

Releasing a deep sigh, she looks heavenward as if practicing patience with me.

"You know, Cat Lady came by today."

Ugh. Cat Lady is our snarky term for our landlord. No one else in the entire apartment building is allowed to have pets, but she's got a veritable menagerie in her place. I'm one week overdue on the rent, and she's not gonna be happy.

"She says we're overdue," Bailey says. "And then when she realized you weren't home, she started in about calling Child Protective Services. Says it's illegal." Bailey frowns. "I might be tiny and short, but it doesn't mean I'm not capable of watching us."

"Of course, you are," I tell her. "And I'll have her rent money on Friday." Desperation claws at my belly, angry and fierce. She came when I wasn't here on purpose and threatened my siblings. I hate her. I hate my mother for putting us through this. I hate myself for not holding us together.

But I will.

The proposition niggles in the back of my mind. I can't sell myself to keep us together. Bailey wouldn't want that.

Do I have to sell myself? Or can I make it a game? No no no no no no no.

It's kinky prostitution.

"She said tomorrow, or she'll tell the police."

I sigh. "Of course, she did." She doesn't have the right to evict us quite yet, but legally I've been late so many times on the rent, she can make my life a living hell.

"I tried to call you," Bailey says, "but it just went to voicemail."

"Will we have to go to a shelter?" Ben asks, his voice trembling.

"*No,*" I tell him emphatically. "And Bailey, I couldn't call you or take your call because my phone is broken." I groan. "I need to replace it." But how the hell can I replace it when rent is overdue?

"Oh boy," Bailey says with a groan.

I run a hand across my forehead and close my

eyes. "I'll figure something out, guys. I promise. Just eat your dinner and get your homework done, okay? I've got to get to work."

"When do you have time to take care of *you*, Cora?" Bailey asks softly. "You look like you haven't had a decent night's sleep in weeks. I hear you, up at night, doing your homework when we've gone to bed. Studying, typing. You get no sleep and you're running on fumes."

"I know," I say, shaking my head to dismiss her concerns. "I'm fine, honey. This is what people do in college."

The lie sounds foolish even to me. This is what people do in college? Work two jobs and get no sleep so they can keep their families together? Or do they get drunk at frat parties and lose their virginity?

It doesn't matter. None of it really matters. All that matters is that I'm doing the best I can to hold us together.

I go to my room and get dressed for Verge.

I need a phone.

I need to pay rent.

I need some rest.

And I need to get Liam Alexander out of my mind.

I whisper a silent prayer. Until recently, this all seemed so possible. So promising.

And now all I've got is a proposition from an asshole to sell myself to him like a fucking whore.

But as I sit in the car on the way to Verge, my mind begins to wander.

What would it mean to be his submissive for eight weeks?

What would he expect of me?

No one ever needs to know…

I shake my head when I get out at the club. I can't let myself be swayed by this temptation. I make my way to the entrance, I knock, then smile at Geoff when he answers.

"Cora. Nice to see you."

"Hey. How's Giada doing? I heard she was under a major deadline and no one's seen her."

"She's good," he says. "But am I ever ready for her to get this book in already. I've hardly seen her." Giada is his girlfriend, and she's a writer. Occasionally she gets caught under a deadline and goes missing for days at a time, totally consumed with her work. Geoff puts up with it, and even though he grumbles, he's proud of her. We all are. She and Chandra are excellent writers, and I love when we get to display their new books at Marla's store.

"How are you?" he asks. And there's something in his tender tone that makes a lump rise in my throat. I'm so wound up, someone I hardly know has me near tears with the most common of pleasantries.

"I'm good," I say, ducking my head so he doesn't see the tears well in my eyes. "Gotta get to work." I step quickly past him and nearly collide into Braxton and Zoe in the waiting area.

"I'm not gonna do it," she says. "No way, no how."

"Do what?" I ask. Zoe's standing with her hands on her hips squaring off to Braxton. She's little, but the girl's a spitfire.

"A demonstration," Zoe says, her black hair falling on her forehead when she looks at me. "The people scheduled to demonstrate tonight are sick, and everyone's come here for a show." She waves a hand in the direction of the bar entrance behind her. "It's *full* in there."

"Who was scheduled to demonstrate what?"

"Beatrice and Zack were demonstrating the flogger," Zoe supplies. "But Beatrice got a stomach bug, and you know Zack. He doesn't scene with anyone else, *ever*. So Brax is trying to talk me into it, and a public demonstration is just not my thing." My pulse races at the sound of the word *flogger*. It sounds terrible. Flogging is like a hard whipping or something, right? Zoe gives Brax a coy look. "Not to mention the fact that I enjoy the flogger on bare skin, and that ain't happening in front of anyone else."

Is she mad?

Brax sighs and looks heavenward, shaking his head.

"Aww. Well I'm sure Tobias will find someone." I feel bad for Zoe but can't imagine doing something like that myself.

"Find someone to do what?"

No.

I know that voice, and I want him to leave. A petty, juvenile part of me wants to take my ball and go home.

I was here first!

My skin prickles at the sound of the familiar voice behind me, and when I turn, there he is. No longer in his suit, he's wearing black club attire, bare, tattooed arms folded across his chest, feet planted apart. Tonight, he isn't wearing a mask, though, and he's staring right at me.

"Cora," he greets with a nod.

"Liam," I respond coolly.

"Oh, hey, Liam," Zoe says, like he's just some guy who dropped by for a drink and not *Liam Alexander,* filthy rich asshole and dream destroyer.

"Hey," he says with a nod.

Brax explains. "Tobias had a demonstration planned tonight, and people have been looking forward to it, but Beatrice is sick, and Zack won't scene with just anyone. I was trying to convince Zoe to do it with me." He rolls his eyes at her. "And she's not into it." He mutters under his breath, "But if she continues being so ornery, we'll have a *private* session soon."

Zoe's cheeks flush a little and she juts her chin out but doesn't respond.

"What type of demonstration?" Liam drawls in that sexy voice of his.

Oh my God. He is not considering this! I can't... I won't... *just no.* Demonstrations usually take place in the dungeon, I think? But the thought of him wielding a flogger on another girl...

Why does that bother me?

Ha. It doesn't. I'm just wound up from today.

But it does.

"Flogger," Brax says. "And it's no free will offering, either. Tobias has been promoting demonstrations, and the turnout tonight's pretty solid. There's a damn good payout for the demo."

A payout? They're paying someone?

Hold the phone.

"I'll do it," Liam says. "Take me to Tobias?"

Zoe and I share a wide-eyed stare when the men walk into the bar area together.

"What does he think he's doing?" I hiss at Zoe.

Shrugging, she just smiles. "Liam's an expert top," she says. "Didn't you know that? He's an old friend of Tobias'. I'm just a little surprised he's interested in doing a demonstration, because he's typically very private."

Of course he is.

Is he doing this just to show off for me? What the hell?

"C'mon," Zoe says. "I could use a drink, and you're the woman for the job."

Why does it bother me so much that Liam's considering this? I have no claim on him. He's made a ridiculous proposition, and one I'm not super into agreeing to. But as I walk to the bar and wrap an apron around my mid-section, I think about his proposition.

What exactly would it entail? God, I could use that money.

I greet Travis in a sort of haze, my mind preoccupied. Pulling drinks, wiping down the counter, refilling the little bowls of roasted nuts. I do my job like an automaton, barely registering what I'm doing.

Could I scene with Liam? Hell, all he did was take me over his lap for a pretty tame spanking, and he made me climax. What would it really be like scening with him?

Tobias approaches the bar and Travis hands him a drink.

"Find anyone to demo yet, Tobias?" I ask, feigning nonchalance. Travis gives me a sidelong look I don't miss. My voice is unnaturally high-pitched and shaky.

"Got a top," Tobias says. "Liam's offered to demonstrate. Still looking for a bottom, though. I would have thought people would leap at a chance to scene with a guy like him, but I think people find him intimidating."

Oh, really? I think to myself. *Good looks, filthy rich, and a dom. What's intimidating about that?*

How about the fact that he's an asshole?

I look around the room. It really *is* pretty busy here tonight, busier than usual, and I notice the pool tables and circular tables and chairs have all moved to the side so there's a wide-open wall in front of us.

"Why is the room all rearranged?" I ask Tobias.

"For the demonstration that might not happen," Tobias responds, sipping his drink. "We decided to do a demonstration here rather than the Dungeon, because people complained demonstrations in the dungeon detracted from play."

"Ah. Well, that makes sense," I say, and I'm surprised I can talk at all given that my mouth is dry and feels like it's been stuffed with cotton.

Liam steps onto the floor, wielding a wicked looking tool in his hand, crimson red with strips of leather.

Oh my God. *That's* the flogger.

"Are floggers super painful?" I ask quietly.

"Nah," Travis says. "The name makes it sound wicked, but it's pretty tame. It can produce a good sting, and not all floggers are the same, but it's a good beginner's implement."

"Really?" I say, my voice weirdly squeaky.

"That's why I chose it for tonight's demonstration," Tobias says. "So we can dispel some myths about floggers. Newcomers think they're brutal, but they rarely are. I mean, like Travis said, you definitely can work up a good sting with one, but they're nowhere near as intense as a leather strap or tawse."

I pull a few more drinks and hand them out, smiling at the patrons who come for a drink, but I'm a million miles away.

Liam's giving a demonstration. They need someone willing to receive the pain. *And there's a payout.*

I pour a drink for a customer, and as I hand it to him, Liam approaches the bar. I open my mouth to say something, then realize he didn't come to speak to me but Tobias. Nervously, I turn away, and accidentally knock the glass of whiskey over and it spills all over a guy sitting at the bar.

"Oh my God, I'm so sorry," I say, heat creeping up my neck, I'm so embarrassed.

"Hey!" the guy says, jumping back from the bar. I grab a bar mop. "Stupid bitch," he mutters. "Got me wet."

My cheeks flame with indignation. He did *not!*

But before I can say a thing to defend myself, Liam's got the guy by the back of the shirt, pulling him straight out of his chair like he's a child.

No way. I blink in surprise.

"What did you call her?" he says in a dangerous tone. My heart thuds in my chest. What the hell is going on here? Liam gives the guy a shake.

The man is like half Liam's size, though to be fair, it seems most guys are, because he's freaking huge. The man squirms and tries to get away. "Hey!" he yells to Tobias. "No one's allowed to manhandle anyone. You're the owner. Do something!"

"You violated the rules of conduct first," Tobias says coolly. Travis stands next to me with his arms crossed on his chest, glaring at the jerk.

Ok, so, I really love it here.

"I believe you owe the lady an apology," Liam

says, in a "make my day" tone of voice that, to my dismay, actually makes my heart skip a beat.

No one's ever defended me before.

No one.

Ever.

Why does it have to be this jerk?

"I'm sorry," the guy mumbles. "Now let me go."

"Will you ever speak to the lady like that again?" He gives him another shake.

"No," the guy says. "Let me go!"

"I think it's time for you to go home," Tobias says. "Liam, escort him?"

"Happily," Liam says, dragging the guy away from the bar by his collar.

They're gone. I look to Tobias and Travis.

"Thanks, guys," I say.

Travis jerks his chin up, then goes to the other side of the bar to take drink orders. Tobias turns to me.

"Good man, Liam," he says. That's when I remember that Liam and Tobias are long-term friends.

"I forgot you knew each other," I say. I have so many questions I want to ask, but I don't want to pry.

"Yeah, we go way back," Tobias says, taking another sip from his drink. Turning away from me, he frowns at the growing crowd in the room. "No chance you're game for a demo, Cora?" He's half-joking but seems nearly desperate. "Can't believe I can't find a single woman to bottom for Liam

Alexander. And the payout's not bad, if I don't say so myself."

"So, um, what's the payout?" I ask.

Tobias tells me and I nearly drop the glass I'm holding. "For real?"

"For real."

"Well, shit," I mutter, wiping down the counter. "If I didn't have to work tonight, I would so do it."

What did I just say? What the hell is *wrong* with me? I start wiping the counter at a breakneck speed.

"That's not a problem," Tobias says. "I can cover this shift during your demo. Hell, I'd love it if you'd demonstrate with him. Then we wouldn't have to disappoint anyone, and I know you're levelheaded enough you won't ruin the scene."

Oh my God, I can't believe I'm doing this.

Better than being his *sub*.

One scene? That I can do.

I'm insane.

"Who's ruining the scene?" Liam joins us at the bar again, looking at Tobias, not me.

"No one," Tobias says. "In fact, we're all set. Cora's agreed to demo with you."

I swear I shiver when he swivels those fierce eyes of his back to me.

"Um," I mumble, before I lose my resolve. "I... I've just agreed to do the demo with you." Right. Tobias just said that. I'm brilliant.

Like, don't you even think I'm taking you up on that proposition, mister.

He eyes me so coldly, I fear he'll reject me, and suddenly the knowledge that he can makes my heart hurt a little.

"Sounds good," he says, his face impassive, save the faintest little twitch in his jaw. "But first, we talk in my private room."

"Um, sure?"

I move without really thinking, stepping away from the bar, suddenly not so sure about this decision. Liam grasps my elbow firmly, marching me away from the bar to the private rooms down the hall. Is he angry? What the hell?

To my right, I hear the sound of people in the dungeon, but everything seems so far away and muted, as my blood pounds in my ears. I'm so wound up, suddenly nervous as fuck.

I just agreed to let Liam flog me? In front of a room full of people? The look on his face and grip on my arm tell me that just royally pissed him off.

Good.

Jerk.

He sticks a key into a navy-colored door, opens it, and practically shoves me in, slamming the door shut behind him.

"Liam, what are you—?" But I don't get any further, because in one rapid tug, he shoves me up against the wall, caging me in with an arm on either side of me. My heart stutters in my chest with the way he's looking at me, like he wants to rip me apart with his bare hands. Damn, he smells good. It isn't even fair. Those sapphire eyes are alight with fire, and he's breathing heavily, as if he's trying to keep himself in check.

"What the *fuck* do you think you're playing at?" he asks in a growl.

"What are *you* doing?" I try to shove him off me, but he's big and strong and it's like trying to move a brick wall.

His strong fingers grasp my chin so I can't look away. "I don't play games, Cora," he says, "I do *not* play games."

"I don't— I didn't mean—"

And then his mouth is on mine, and I can't think straight, can't move, because I'm immobilized. I'm losing control of my body because my knees are buckling, but he's holding me against him, so hard and yet so gentle all at the same time. The kiss is punishing, bruising my lips with its intensity. His fingers rake through hair, a delicious, erotic tug, and my mouth opens further for him.

I moan with the loss when he pulls his mouth off mine and whispers in my ear. "No fucking games, Cora."

"No games," I promise. "It's just one night."

He nips my ear then pulls the lobe between his teeth and suckles. Shivers race up and down my spine.

"Then why did you say yes, if not to fuck with me? To tease me with what I can't have?" He towers over me, and with me pinned against the wall, I feel the size difference between us so keenly. His eyes blaze into mine like blue fire, the heat skating down my whole body and thrumming between my thighs.

"No," I say, shaking my head at him. "I didn't do that. I wouldn't. God, Liam, why would I do that?"

"I don't know," he says. "Why *would* you? If you didn't do it to get back at me, why did you agree?"

I swallow hard, tamping down my pride. It matters to me that he doesn't think I'm playing him. I value authenticity. So, I give him the truth.

"I need the money," I say in a small, trembling voice, so mad at myself that I can't keep my shit together. "I... I'm behind on rent. Any minute now, they'll shut off our electricity. And I need a new damn phone after those jerks busted mine."

"I offered you money," he counters. "And you were too damned proud to take it."

"You didn't offer me *money*. And it wasn't pride," I protest. "It's... more than that."

Was it?

A knock sounds at the door before he gets a chance to reply.

"Liam? Time for the demo." Sounds like Braxton.

"We'll be right there."

He grasps my chin between his index finger and thumb. "Club safeword, babe," he says, but the *babe* rings with sarcasm.

"Oh, I know the safeword," I tell him. "Loud and clear, *babe*."

The sadistic grin he gives me makes me inwardly groan.

Oh, so smart, mouthing off to the man who's about to whip your ass.

EIGHT

Liam

IF SHE HAD any idea how badly I can't wait to flog her sweet, saucy little ass, she wouldn't be throwing sass at me like confetti.

The nerve of the woman scorning my proposition, then pairing up with me for a demonstration I can't get out of.

Lucky for her, it's just the flogger and not a more intense implement, but *hell* if she doesn't she need a harder implement. I've never met a more obstinate woman in my life.

Still. I'll control this scene. And I can have fun with the flogger.

"Should I get dressed into something else?" she asks, suddenly paling when I take her by the hand.

"You've got something to change into?" I ask.

"Well. Um. No," she says.

I don't want her to think I'm laughing at her, so I keep my face straight. "Well, then, I don't think that's an option." I like holding her little hand in mine as we walk toward the demo area. "And there's no fucking way I'm doing this scene with you naked." I'd kill any motherfucker who laid eyes on her naked. God, what am I doing? I want to haul her ass back to my room and lock the door.

"I look silly, though," she protests.

I give her a sidelong glance. "You look beautiful." And she does, with her gorgeous vibrant hair, vivid eyes, pale, freckled cheeks, and lips still swollen after that kiss I gave her. What I would give to explore every inch of those beautiful curves of hers.

As soon as I tell her she's beautiful, I regret it. *God,* what is my problem? She is nothing at all like what I want in a woman. She's nothing but trouble. But damn if I can't get this girl out of my mind.

"Okay, guys," Brax says, standing by as tonight's dungeon monitor. "Let's go over the rules."

I feel Cora tense beside me, so I squeeze her hand but keep my eyes fixed on Brax.

"Cora, club safeword?"

"Apple," she says.

Brax nods. "When scening at Verge, we insist couples begin with a safeword of their own, or at least a discussion of the club safeword. Everyone know what that is?"

A loud chorus of, "Apple" goes up and someone whines, "Aw, man, just when things were getting fun."

Brax smiles but shakes his head. "We can laugh about it, but it's no joking matter. Sometimes in the middle of a scene, emotions run high. Even with someone you trust, sometimes things can get a little too heated in the moment. A safeword doesn't always have to mean a scene ends, but it can be a pause so that the people scening can communicate. Safewording isn't something anyone should be ashamed of."

People nod all around the room. I watch Cora's reaction. She doesn't make eye contact with me, and her hand is cold in mine, trembling a little. I hope Brax finishes up soon, before she loses her resolve.

I give Brax a chin lift, a silent, "Finish it up, man."

"Okay, take the floor, Liam."

It's unusual for me to do anything like this, to put myself in the spotlight. As a businessman, I like to keep things private. I never scene here without a mask, but tonight, I'm feeling reckless. Maybe it's because she ran out on me and it angered me. Or maybe it's because I think she's afraid, and I don't want to give in to my own fears. To somehow show her that there's nothing to be afraid of.

Or maybe I don't want anything between the two of us when I take these strips of leather to her ass.

Brax steps to the side, and I take Cora in one hand and the flogger in another. Standing in front of the crowd, I take her chin between my fingers and lift her eyes to mine.

"What's your safeword, sweetheart?" I ask, loud and clear for the room to hear, now that a hush has fallen.

"Apple, sir," she says like a good little submissive.

Jesus, I want her. And I'm not above negotiations. So tonight, I'm going to show her exactly what she's leaving on the table.

"Good girl," I tell her approvingly. "You know your safeword, and you know when to use it?"

Nodding, she whispers, "Yes, sir."

Still holding her chin, I lower my mouth to hers and brush a gentle kiss to her lips, then whisper in her ear. "You won't need to safeword with me, Cora." I continue to whisper in her ear while I drag the vibrant red tails of leather over her shoulder, down her back, and across her upper thighs wishing it was her bare skin.

I address the crowd while caressing the leather over every inch of her. "The flogger can be used to produce so many different sensations, from a tickle to a searing lash that raises welts. Some are more severe than others. I tend to like a moderate one, like this." I hold it up to the crowd. "It delivers a solid sting, but it isn't severe. It can be very sensual, and functions as an excellent warm-up implement for a session, but also suitable for a nice, lengthy scene. Unlike more severe implements, the flogger is suitable to be used over other parts of the body as well." I dangle it over her shoulders then breast, enjoying the way she shudders, and when I get to her ass, I bring it back and flick her hard with it once, twice, three times.

Cora gasps and holds onto me tighter, and a low murmur skitters through the crowd. "These are excellent for travel, and many can even be carried in a pocket. However, beware that these implements are loud." I give Cora a smile. "And your submissive might be, too."

The crowd laughs appreciatively.

Now it's time to dom her.

I step back and point the flogger toward the wall that's waiting for us. "Flogging can be done with the submissive in pretty much any position. Tied with back bared on a St. Andrew's Cross. Back down, breasts up, so you can flog her front. Over a spanking bench for a more thorough whipping. And because of the relative short size of the flogger, over the knee works as well. For tonight, we'll have her present herself for her punishment facing the wall."

Facing the wall, her hands tremble when she places them palm down. Gently, I kick her legs apart and begin the lecture for the sake of entertainment.

"Was it fair for you to raise your voice to me, little one?" I ask, pacing behind her with the flogger in hand, while I tap it on my palm.

"No, sir," she says with mock repentance.

There are oh so many things she needs to be punished for.

"Let's see...I think we have quite a list of infractions. You've stormed away from me, mouthed off, talked back..."

"I didn't exactly—"

"Interrupted me and proven my point with the backtalk."

Shaking my head, I rear back and swing the flogger through the air, giving her a good, hard smack. She gasps but keeps position.

"Is that proper behavior?"

"No, sir," she says, giving me a discreet sidelong look. Her eyes are bright and curious. Leaning in, I take her chin between my thumb and forefinger.

"What do you deserve for this?"

"I... I deserve to be punished, sir."

"You do." I take my position behind her and flick my wrist. The lengths of leather falls on her ass with a satisfactory *snap*. Addressing the crowd, I bring my arm back again. "You can administer tame strokes of the flogger. They work very well as a sort of warm-up." In silence, I administer half a dozen gentler strokes, criss-crossing her pert ass. "Or," I explain to the crowd. "You can administer much more punishing strokes." This time, I bring the flogger searing through the air with a whistle, and I know I've met my mark when she cries out from the sting of the lashes. I pause, but she doesn't issue a safeword, so I continue, slow, steady lashes of the flogger, covering her fully clothed upper thighs and ass with the firm, heated strokes.

At twenty strokes, she's relaxed, and is fully immersed into the scene, her eyes closed and her breathing slow and steady.

"The varying strokes of the flogger are excellent for coaxing your submissive to sub-space," I say to the crowd. "Varied pain and pleasure are what heighten the response that will bring your submissive to the edge of utter bliss. Start slowly, with gentler strokes." I demonstrate. "Then harder, with a whip-like motion of your wrist." A few more hard swats fall, but she barely flinches this time.

In silence, I work the flogger, hard and fast, getting fucking hard at the sound of her little cries and moans. If I pulled down her panties and swept my fingers through her, she'd be soaked.

"It helps to massage out pain," I say, squeezing and massaging her flaming hot ass. "And it also mitigates any bruising. Sometimes, however," I explain. "Submissives do far better knowing this is punishment, and there is no comforting reward when they're being punished."

I shrug. "But Cora's a good girl who just needs a firm hand. Come here, Cora." I'm not playing anymore, and she knows it.

Tucking the flogger into my pocket, she turns to me with wide, curious eyes. I cup her cheek in my hand and kiss her forehead. "You were a very good girl for our demonstration." I speak louder, to be heard above the noise of the crowd. "Have you learned your lesson?"

I know she's acting. I know this isn't really who she is. But when she lowers her lashes and nods her head quietly, I can't help but kiss her once more. We're not playing anymore, because now her head is on my shoulder and she's wrapped up in my arms. I'm hoisting her into the air and holding her against me, her head falling into the hollow of my neck as if she's meant to be there. She's relaxed and soft, and feels nice nestled against my chest like this, and I need to get her alone now.

"Any questions?" I ask. Cora sighs, her eyes closed, and doesn't even register the sound of voices.

"What types of floggers are the more serious ones?" Someone asks. "How do you know?"

I hold the flogger up to show. "The different types of strands here—falls, they're called—vary in length, weight, and material. Most floggers are made with leather, but some are not. A softer, suede-like leather will produce a gentler sensation, whereas harder, sturdier material will pack a greater punch. Keep in mind, though, that a flogger is a versatile tool, because unlike other implements, the sensation can be either whippy or thuddy."

"Whippy or thuddy?" someone asks. Cora burrows deeper into my chest. I need to get her out of here.

"Whippy like a whip, thuddy like a paddle." It's a basic fact of impact play and I won't offer any more details, because my job here is done. I don't offer to answer any more questions either. "Thank you, everyone. She needs some aftercare and *that* I prefer to be private." A tall, black-haired guy in leather is scoping Cora out, and I feel my body tense. I don't want anyone else to look at her. I've marked her and made her mine, and the rest of them can go to hell.

I turn my back to him and ignore the rest of them, marching with Cora in my arms like I'm carrying the victory flag in battle.

NINE

Cora

I'M FLOATING, soaring, as if he's awoken every nerve-ending I have. This can't be the cold, distant rich guy who's been giving me shit. This is... this man is tender. Skillful. Somehow, bringing out the dominant in him has brought out the very best.

I don't want him to let me go. I want to stay like this wrapped up in his arms forever.

"I'll never fucking do that again," he growls in my ear.

"Do what?" I ask, but my words feel slurred, like I'm drunk or half asleep. The door slams shut and before I know what's happening, I'm flat on my back and he's over me, nearly smothering me, the scent of whiskey and leather and expensive cologne filling my senses. I blink, trying to adjust my eyes to the dim light overhead, but it seems too bright.

"Do what?" he repeats, his tone furious. "Do anything in public with you again."

"But that was... hot," I mumble.

"Fuck hot."

Is the staid business man... jealous?

"Double, Cora."

I blink in confusion at him. "Double what? What are you talking about?"

"My offer earlier today," he says, and I suddenly realize he's stripping out of his clothes and *Christ Almighty* he's beautiful. Wide, muscled shoulders, his chest thick and broad with defined muscles that bunch when he moves with fluid grace.

"You need the money," he says. "Don't fucking lie to me." His eyes are alight with blue fire, the molten look he's giving me searing me in place with its heat.

"I do," I whisper, and weirdly, the words conjure up wedding vows and white lacy dresses and it both exhilarates and terrifies me. My nerve endings are on overdrive, so sensitized I feel like I'm on the verge of both laughing and crying. "I do. But I'll manage."

"Fuck manage," he says, then he's got my wrists in his hand, pinning them over my head, and he's on top of me, knees straddling my torso so firmly I'm pinned in place.

I want him to fuck me, and the notion absolutely shocks me.

"Eight weeks?" I repeat. "I have questions, though. I'm not gonna be your whore, Liam."

He shakes his head. "I get that. If I wanted a whore, I wouldn't have come here."

"I'm not giving you everything," I tell him. "Not like some doms want. I have...standards."

"Of course," he says, "And doms come from every walk of life and want many different things, you know."

"So do subs," I say quickly.

"Exactly."

I don't even know the terms of the contract, but I can't say no. The man I saw during the demonstration wasn't the angry, scornful asshole, but a passionate, skilled man with fierce protective instincts.

The kind of man I need.

The kind of man I crave.

"Who are you?" I ask him. "The man who scoffs or the man who protects?"

"Both, sweetheart. I'm both."

"I want this," I tell him. "Because fucking hell, Liam, I want both."

I'm wrapped in his arms and his mouth is on mine as if he's dying for air and I'm his oxygen. He's sucking me in, consuming me, and I feel as if he's just undone me. Like I was laced up tighter than a corset and he's tugged me free. I'm floating, free fall, and it's exhilarating and terrifying, but I can't imagine anything more perfect. With crazed, nearly angry tugs and tears, he undresses me, my clothing falling to the floor in a messy tumble.

"Rule number one, you get tested," he says. "And I show you mine."

"Okay," I tell him, my body humming with wild need.

I watch as he slides down to the floor, kneeling in front of me. Lifting my hot, sore ass in his hands he lowers his mouth to my sex.

"Oh my God."

"Rule number two," he growls, his heated breath gracing my inner thighs. "You come only when I tell you."

I whimper when he drags his tongue along my inner thigh.

"Liam," I groan. "Oh God."

"Open your legs, sweetheart," he orders. I hesitate, not knowing what he'll do, and he doesn't like my hesitation. "Now, Cora, or I'll flog you again."

"Mmm," I groan with the memory of the spanking he just gave me. I open my legs and welcome him, my eyes closing in utter bliss when he doesn't even hesitate but swipes his tongue through my swollen folds. With deliberate movements, he nips and suckles, teasing my clit and licking his way down until he plunges his tongue at my entrance. It's fucking dirty and hot as hell, and I need more. Harder. Longer. Then he traces his way back up again to my clit, teasing and suckling.

I freeze when I feel his fingers at my asshole,

but he slaps my outer thigh. "You safeword if you need to," he says. "But I control this now."

I shake my head.

"No one's every touched me there…please don't stop."

"That's my girl," he groans against my inner thigh. "*Fuuuck*, you taste so damn good I don't ever want to forget this." He touches every part of me with probing fingers, while he sucks and laps at my folds. I'm drowning in ecstasy, already so near to climaxing.

"Now," he says. "When you're ready, you come on my mouth, baby."

Oh, sweet *Jesus,* that's all I need. I buck and moan as I topple over into ecstasy, writhing so hard he has to hold me down on the bed, and when I'm finally spent, he stands and strokes his cock.

"Christ, you're beautiful when you come," he says, groaning as he strokes his swollen cock harder, faster. I get on my knees and reach for him, begging him to let me do this with a silent plea. One nod, and he releases his cock. I swallow, eager to touch him. To please him.

"Fuuuuuuck," he groans. I'm kneeling with him in front of me, jerking his cock into my breasts.

"Baby," he groans, then he mutters a string of tortured curse words before his body tenses and I know he's gonna come.

"Please mark me, sir." I whisper, jerking his cock harder, faster.

His hips jerk while he spills his seed on me,

scorching hot liquid coursing down my breasts while he groans his release. He leans his forehead to mine and holds me to him, panting. We're a mess and I don't care. The look of utter bliss in his eyes before he came was my reward.

Finally, he slumps against me and gently eases my hand off of him.

"Shower," he groans. "Now."

I gladly join him. It's surreal, the two of us like this, still shaking from the intensity of the scene. I'm naked and marked by him, suddenly not so eager to get clean, still drunk on the intimacy we shared.

"C'mere," he says, after he's put the shower on. And as steam billows around us, he tugs me close to him in an embrace so tight it's almost painful. Taking me by the hand, he leads me into the shower and holds my hand so I don't fall.

In silence, he lathers a washcloth and cleans me, with the tenderness that belies his stern exterior. When he's done, I soap his back and chest.

"So, tell me, Liam Alexander," I finally say. "What exactly happens now?"

TEN

Liam

I MAKE her wait until we're out of the shower, still damp and wrapped in towels, before we go into the main room.

"Do you remember rule number one?" I ask her.

"Yeah. We both get tested and show each other the results. Fair enough. I'm clean."

"Good. And you take birth control."

"Easy enough. I already do." She nods and sits on the edge of the bed.

"Rule number two, no climaxing until I tell you."

"Got it."

"Rule number three." This one may give her pause. "You obey me, or I punish you."

I watch as she bites her lip and looks away. "Like. Obey you about *what?*"

I could've predicted this. But there is no submissive contract without obedience.

"Everything."

"Everything?" She squeaks. "Like if you said, *I don't like those shoes, get another pair*, I have to listen?"

"Precisely. Though typically my directions will be a lot less superfluous and will focus on our relationship more than your private life."

Her brow furrows while she looks at me, her pretty lips turning down into a frown.

"Wait a minute," she says. "Are you going to use this contract to get me to stop my crusade against your company? Are you tricking me?"

I nearly roll my eyes. As if I think her little tantrum over my building projects are going to make a dent in my plans.

"You can crusade all you want, sweetheart. We'll keep business separate from pleasure."

"You promise?"

"I promise. I may be an asshole, but I'm a man of my word."

"Right," she says, nodding. "And if you punish me," she continues with a furrowed brow. "What exactly might that entail? Because frankly, I mean, not to shoot myself in the foot or anything, but that flogging and that spanking were pretty hot. It's not exactly punishment."

"I can punish you however I see fit," I tell her.

"Though I must confess, I definitely prefer a good spanking. The only reason you liked the other spankings was because I made them likable."

"Really," she says with a raised brow and a little snort. "Not sure I believe you."

Taking her wrist, I tug her over to me and divest her of her towel. "Care for a demonstration?" I ask, her hesitation is answer enough. I quickly push her over my knee and give her a series of rapid spanks on her bare ass, the wet skin magnifying the sound and intensity.

"Ohhh, ow!" she hollers. "Got it. Yep."

Standing her upright, I hand her her towel.

"Well. Fine, then," she says, her adorable freckled cheeks flushed pink. "Yeah, okay. So, I'm sure I won't really disobey you *that* much, and if punishment is just an over-the-knee spanking, I'll deal."

"Could be other things."

"Like what?" she asks warily.

"Orgasm denial. Anal plug. Things like that."

"Things like that," she repeats, a little breathless. "Well then."

"Rule number four," I continue, as I go get a change of clothes from the wardrobe I keep in here. "Sex whenever, wherever I want."

"Are you a exhibitionist?" she asks so seriously it's almost cute.

"No. I'm a jealous, possessive fucker," I tell her, which actually makes her laugh.

"Then why'd you do the demo?"

"Tobias is my friend."

"So no getting it on in the middle of Times Square. Good," she says. "I look forward to rule number four."

My bark of laughter seems to startle her, for she jumps, and her cheeks flush a pretty pink. She's already nearly earned the money I'll pay her.

"Typically, with number five, I make the submissive live with me for the duration of our contract, but since that's an impossibility with you, I'll demand that you have things here in the private room that you can use if necessary. Is it ever possible for you to get a babysitter?"

"Well," she says thoughtfully. "Yeah. We've got a neighbor I trust in our building who will check in on Bailey and Ben, but they're pretty independent. I just definitely prefer being home at night with them."

"Fair enough," I say. "So, some nights, I'll stay at your place."

"God, no," she says, her face paling. Does she dislike the idea of her siblings meeting me? That troubles me somehow. But she continues, and her answer surprises me. "I... I don't ever want you to come inside my home, Liam."

I shake my head. "If that's what you want, okay. It won't be anything I haven't seen before," I press.

"No. Please, no."

I shrug. "Alright, then, if it matters that much to

you. Some nights we stay here, though, in my private room."

"Thank you," she whispers. "That I can agree to, if my neighbor can watch the kids. Any more rules?"

I nod. "You *always* have your cell phone with you when we're apart so that I can text or call you when I need to."

"Um, problem," she says, flushing. "I... don't have one, remember?"

I swear under my breath. "Right. I'll get you one."

"You don't have to get me one," she protests. "I'm getting paid for that demonstration tonight, and I—"

"I'm getting you a cell phone, and that's the end of this discussion."

"But if I—"

"But if you finish that sentence after we've signed the contract, I'll punish you."

Training her will be so rewarding. She's a feisty little one, but she enjoys her punishment. It's the perfect combination.

"Right," she says. "Wow, this is gonna be tough."

I shrug. "I'll ease you into it."

But she shakes her head. "How? I think I'll mess up every few seconds and end up in a state of constant punishment."

What she'll end up in is a state of constant arousal, but I think she'll like it.

"This is all very Fifty Shades," she mutters.

"Fifty what?" I ask.

"Oh, you're funny," she says. "As if you don't know what I'm talking about."

Of course, I do, but it's fun to tease her. "Cora, I've been doing this since Christian Fucking Grey was in diapers."

Her snort of laughter makes me smile. "So, you've done this many times, then."

"Yes."

"I have... well. I have one more question," she finally blurts out, but she doesn't meet my eyes. I won't allow her to hide from me and looking into her eyes is the best way for me to really read her. And as her almost-dominant, I need to be able to see those eyes. Reaching for her chin, I draw her gaze to mine.

"Look at me, Cora. I want your eyes on me. There is no hiding in this."

"I know," she whispers. "You're different when you're the dom. You know that?"

I shake my head. "I'm always the dom. I'm no different here than I am anywhere else."

Placing her hand on my arm, her voice gentles as she continues. "You are," she says. "Out there, you're the boss, yeah. You like things to go your way. But when you're the dom? And you're scening or even talking with me? You lose that edge. You lose that anger you wield like a weapon. There's a nurturing side of you that only comes out when you're being the dom."

I take a breath so deep.

"You make it easy," I confess. I need to change the subject. "You said you had a question."

"I do." Swallowing, she inhales then exhales, letting her breath out slowly. "Out there," she says, her voice dropping to just above a whisper. "After you scened with me. You were... tender. You gave me aftercare. Will I get aftercare like that when we scene?"

I don't answer her at first but lay her back on the bed so she's beneath me. The towel falls to the side, her damp hair scattered on the pillow, curly damp tendrils I want to weave around my fingers. My mouth to her ear, my body flush against hers I whisper. "Always."

"Then I'm not so sure I'll be able to obey you, Liam. Oh. Should I call you sir?"

"When we're scening, yes. But I like hearing you say my name. And you will indeed wish to obey me by the time we're through. You'll see."

"I don't like that I'm predictable."

God, no. I shake my head and hold her to me. "Sweetheart, you're anything but predictable. I'm just confident this will work well for us."

"You're confident with many things," she whispers. "And Jesus, *fuck,* I want to get those tests done."

"I haven't told you rule number six, though."

"Oh?"

I close my eyes and rest my cheek against hers. "No falling in love, Cora."

"That... won't be a problem," she says with a laugh.

But it's not her I'm worried about.

ELEVEN

Cora

IT'S like I'm trapped in some sort of reality TV show or something, it feels that surreal.

After stating rule number six, Liam pulls away from me and I wish he didn't have to. He made me come no more than half an hour ago, and already my body vibrates with need once more. But I have to get home to Bailey and Ben, and he knows that.

We dress, and it's a little sad, like the curtain falling at the end of a play. And that's what we're doing, isn't it? We're play acting. There's no more authenticity to this than unicorns and mermaids. Whimsical fantasies to distract from the mundane.

But at least I'll be getting paid, and amply.

"Um. So, I get paid at the end of our contract?" I ask, mentally calculating how I'll deal until then.

"No," he says, fastening his belt. "I'll pay you one-third up front. There is no agreement until we've gone over every detail of our contract. I'll have the money wired into your account tomorrow morning. Another third halfway through, and your final payment on the last day of our contract."

Holy *shit*. I can't wait to tell Bailey... though I'll have to tell her in a way that doesn't *really* tell her what's going on.

"Well, that's very generous of you."

"I'll speak with Tobias," he says, dismissing any mention of his generosity. He's a businessman, and this is no act of altruism. "During these two months, I'll cover the salary you'd have earned at Verge."

"Oh, right. You mentioned that in the restaurant. So what are you thinking?"

Turning to me, he shakes his head. "You can't work here while you're with me," he says, and my heart deflates a little. God, I hate that it does. I don't want to let my friends at Verge down. "You'll still come here, but as a guest and not an employee, but only temporarily. I'll talk with Tobias."

"Hmm," I think out loud. "Well, I see your point. But Verge needs a bartender."

"I'll hire one for Tobias."

"You can just do that?" I ask, pulling my top on, and I don't miss the way his eyes grow ravenous. When he swallows, his Adam's apple bobs up and down. I hide a smile so he doesn't see how pleased it makes me that he's affected by my body.

"I do what I want, Cora," he says, but there's no note of pride in his voice. When he turns away from me, he almost looks disgusted with himself.

I don't get it. I'm a curvy girl who can't seem to keep her mouth shut, and he knows how I feel about his company. And as I finish getting dressed, a horrible idea flashes in my mind. Predictably, I voice it since I somehow have lost all ability to filter my thoughts.

"Wait," I tell him. "*Wait.* Are you doing this to try to seduce me so I don't give your company shit about the project you're doing?" I step back from him.

Fuck, I've been had. He's so fucking playing with me. "You are, aren't you?" I ask, shaking my head. "Well you can just—"

"*Stop.*" The sharp tone freezes me. Already I'm responding to his domination and I don't know how I feel about that. Crossing my arms on my chest, I narrow my eyes at him but don't speak.

"I do not mix business with pleasure," he says, his lips pressed into a thin line. "And just so we're clear? Neither do you."

"Oh, right," I huff. "Is that an addendum? Rule number *seven?* You just thought to—"

But I don't finish what I'm saying because in two massive strides he's crossed the room, and his hand's wrapped in my hair, so tightly the words freeze on my lips. I forget what I was even saying when he tugs me against his body. I can feel the tension wound in him, the heat of his breath at my ear.

"No, baby," he whispers. "I don't need to add any fucking *addendums*. Rule number three covers that."

I repeat what he said in my head.

Rule number three: you obey me, or I punish you.

"I've disobeyed you?" I ask, my voice subdued with his grip in my hair.

"I'm not playing you. I'm not seducing you so I can get away with anything. We've already discussed this. What we battle outside of Verge we'll let the lawyers and protests and media handle it. Go ahead. Fight me. I like media coverage. I won't stop you from your little crusade, though I'll tell you now, you're not going to win."

I want to curse him out, but I know that's likely not the smartest move at this juncture. I hate that I find parts of him so compelling and other parts infuriating.

And hell, I need the damn money.

I can play nice at the club.

"Understand?" he asks.

"I think so," I say through gritted teeth. "I can fight you, but you'll win in the end. You won't punish me for trying to stop your company, but it barely ruffles your feathers."

"Well done," he says and in that moment, I hate him. Arrogant fucking *jerk*.

"Now this is what we'll do. We'll talk to Tobias.

I'll tell him what I'd like to do. My driver will take you home tonight, and we'll make plans for you to come to my office to review and sign your contract. Sleep on it."

"Fine," I hiss. The grip in my hair tightens and my eyes water. "Let me go."

He lets me go so quickly, I feel dizzy. Rubbing my scalp, I look at him through eyes that water despite my most valiant effort. "Just so you know?" I say in a wobbly voice. "I like Liam the dom like *fifty times* better than Liam the businessman."

"Fair enough," he says, owning the status of business fucking *prick*.

"Maybe a hundred times better!"

God!

"Let's go to Tobias," he says. I swallow hard.

I want to like the man I'll spend the next two months with. But I can't.

He's only a means to an end.

I'll maintain my control. I'll play it safe. I'll focus on the money that's coming to me and how that will make my life easier.

How funny that he thinks he actually has to give me rule number six.

Fall in love with him? I don't even *like* him.

"Will we have our own safeword?" I ask him. He's straightening up the bed, then picks up his phone and glances at it. When he responds, he's distracted, and I already feel dismissed.

"We don't need our own safeword," he says.

"We're not a real couple. Scening here is good enough, so the club safeword will do."

And somehow, that stings.

It was silly of me to hope that he actually did like me. To even entertain that thought is so damn dangerous, I can't allow myself to go there. He doesn't like me at all, he likes control and a hot little pussy to stick his arrogant dick into.

Whoa. Geez, this guy brings out the most venomous thoughts.

True, though, my inner voice counters.

Is it so bad to be used by a hot guy like him and paid generously? There are a lot worse things I could do for that money and Verge is safe.

Safeish.

Jesus, I need mental help.

"Okay," I tell him. "Apple it is."

Opening the door, he gestures for me to go out first, a bored expression on his face. I exit the room, stepping as far away from him as I can, but in one firm stride, he's got my hand in his massive one, and hell if I don't like how that feels. God, I wish I didn't.

It's okay. Just pretend. Just for now. Enjoy what you can, I tell myself.

So, I do. I walk by his side with my hand in his, painfully aware of every eye on us as we walk past the dungeon and into the main bar area. To my surprise, couples swarm around us like we're celebrities, but Liam dismisses each one with a frown and flick of his palm.

"Not now," he says, like he's used to dealing with paparazzi and news crews. Hell. I guess he is. I catch Travis's eye at the bar, and to my shock, he actually winks at me and gives me a thumbs up. I can't help but giggle at that, which earns me a side-long look of disapproval from Liam, but whatever.

"What's so funny, little girl?" he asks.

"Oh, nothing," I tell him. And it isn't anything, really.

But Tobias isn't in his office. When we reach the front, Liam's car is already waiting.

"I'll talk to Tobias. You go home and get some rest," he instructs. "Your first class tomorrow is when?"

"Ten," I tell him.

"Be in my office by nine," he instructs. "Manuel will take you home. I've just messaged him to come."

Wait. "You're not coming?" I ask. Why does that make my heart sink?

I hate him. I don't need him to escort me anywhere.

"I'm staying here tonight," he says, giving me a look that's cold and distant. "Go home. In the future, when you're in bed, I want you to text me."

"Okayyyyy...But you know, you can't boss me around quite yet," I tell him.

A corner of his lip quirks up, and I can't tell if that's a victory for me or not. I blink in surprise when he sits on the little loveseat in the main lobby and tugs me onto his knee. God, it feels good sitting on his lap, even if I do hate him.

"I'm too heavy for this," I protest. I'm no waif, but he's a pretty big guy. His only response is a sharp crack to my ass.

"Hey!"

"Remember that first night you made a comment about your body, little girl?" He's brushing the hair off my neck. I shiver.

"Liam," I say, and this time I'm pleading. The up and down of my emotions is making me fairly nauseous. "Why do you call me a little girl? I'm not a little girl at all."

"Would you prefer little one?" he asks, the angry edge of his voice gone. Oh, God, I can't take it when he goes all gentle on me. It's so much harder to hate him then.

"Little one?" I ask him. "That's...Well..." my voice trails off. I'm not sure how to respond. I don't know what it is, but it makes me feel... I don't know. Warm and safe and... vulnerable.

"You like it," he says, drawing me to his chest. "Don't you, little one?"

"I do," I admit. "When we... play here... will you call me that?"

"That and so much more," he says. His watch lights up, and too soon, he pushes me gently off his knee.

"Your ride is here." He leads me to the door, and Geoff gives him a chin lift and me a little wave.

"Liam, heard the scene was a hit," he says. "Well done."

"Thank you." The guys chat briefly, before Liam takes me outside.

It means something that the members of Verge respect him. Maybe it's only me he's a jerk around.

And is he even a jerk? Or am I just hardened toward him?

But when he opens the door to the car and instructs Manuel to take me home, I have my answer. He's already looking away with a bored expression.

"Good night," he says. "See you tomorrow. Don't be late for your ride."

He shuts the door and he's gone.

I've imagined any tenderness. This is a business transaction for him, no more, no less.

And that's what I need.

I don't need feelings to complicate my life. This is exactly what I need.

A business transition with clear cut terms.

No strings attached.

I tell myself this over and over. Too many times.

It's nice to get a ride home. The interior of his car is warm, and I like how it makes me feel safe. I'll enjoy the perks of this proposition as long as I can.

The ride is too short, and soon I'm home. I thank Manuel, and before I leave, he says, "I'll be here in the morning to pick you up at 8:45 a.m. Mr. Alexander's orders."

God. I'm so not used to this type of treatment.

"Alright," I tell him. "If he insists."

"That he does."

Of course.

I go upstairs and check on Bailey and Ben, then take a few minutes to tidy up the apartment. I place a few drinking glasses in the dishwasher and wipe down the counters, then get myself ready for bed. And as I do, I replay the scene in the club. I need to remind myself that there's more than money I'll enjoy during this time with him. I can get a good taste of the club scene, and maybe I'll see if it's really for me. And hell, if I didn't enjoy a little of what he has to offer me.

My mind is at war with so many questions, and if I'm honest, fears. What exactly is it that I fear? My mind instantly goes back to *rule number six.*

No falling in love.

I roll my eyes again, even though no one sees me but my ceiling. As *if.*

Yeah, that's not gonna happen. No how, no way.

What is it that I fear, then? I'm really not sure, and I don't want to think about that anymore.

I think about paying my back rent and next month's rent. I think about buying Bailey the clothes that she needs and Ben a new pair of sneakers. I think about going to the grocery store and actually buying some decent food, rather than the cheapest things that will fill our bellies.

I smile to myself. It would be nice to get some real makeup for once. Something that will make me look pretty. And I really should get some clothes if I'm going to be going to Club Verge more often. The day after tomorrow, I have a brief shift at the bookstore, and now I'm looking forward to it. I need Marla and Chandra's advice so damn bad.

I shift on the bed and twist and turn, trying to settle down. I'm both energized and exhausted, and for a brief moment I wish I had my phone so I could text Liam. For some reason, the idea of texting him before bed feels like it would bring a little closure to the night.

I normally fall into bed so tired I can hardly keep my eyes open. And I need rest. But as I lay there, I play over the night.

The sensation of the flogger on my body.

What would it feel like on naked skin?

Liam's mouth between my legs, his skillful tongue making my bones turn to jelly, as he brought me to climax so hard.

What will it feel like to have him inside me?

I'm no virgin, but I've never made love to a man who commands a situation like he does.

The feel of his thumb against my cheek, my jaw cupped in his hand. The smell of leather and grace, the essence of confidence and power. The sound of his breaths mingled with mine, my erratic heartbeat and soft mews.

As my eyes grow heavy with sleep, I make a vow to myself. I'll take what he gives me, the surface level intimacy we'll share for a time. But I will only give him the bare minimum. What I've promised on paper. No more, no less.

I finally fall into a fitful sleep.

"CORA?" Bailey stands in the doorway, dressed for the day, and I hear Ben in the bathroom.

"Morning, honey," I tell her, yawning. The clock tells me it's nearly seven, so I toss off the covers and stretch.

"You okay?" she asks, her head tilted to the side. She's brushing her hair but eyeing me with concern. "You mumbled a lot in your sleep last night."

"Did I?" I suppose it's only natural. I mean, doesn't everyone go to bed thinking about the flogging scene they just had with their future master? I giggle to myself.

"Good to see you smile," she says, with a smile of her own before she heads toward the kitchen. I grab a box of cereal in the kitchen and make myself a cup of coffee, but when I pull the milk out, it's expired. *Damn*. Rifling through the cabinets, I find a loaf of bread, but we're out of butter and jelly.

Today, this will change. I take a deep breath, determined that I won't let this get me down. I've got an opportunity here, and I'm not going to waste it.

"Hey, guys, I've got good news," I tell them. I reach for my purse and take out a few bills. "I got a... special job offer." God, I've got to finalize my story. "And I'll tell you later what it is."

Bailey gives me a curious look while she slides her coat on. "Cora, how can you work another job? Honest to God, you're already—"

"I'm going to figure it out," I tell her. "I promise." I can't tell her I'm not working *for* Verge, though I will be working *at* Verge. "But tonight, we're going to order real pizza, and I'm going to fill you in with all the juicy details."

"*Really*," Bailey says, but all Ben heard was pizza. He whoops and pumps his fist. I hand them the cash and feel kinda proud of myself, shoving away any residual guilt.

"So here," I tell them. "Get yourselves a breakfast sandwich or donut or something on the way to school, okay?"

Bailey takes the money hesitantly. I've taught her too well.

"Okayyy." She says warily. "And yeah, I want details later. *All* the details. Okay?"

"Yeah, sure," I lie. Like hell I'm giving her all the details. "Go, before you're late."

They leave, and I take a frantic look at the time. I've got to move. I grab my schoolbooks and throw them into my bag, then toss my bag on the couch. I plan on taking a quick shower, but then I remember today's day one. Damn it. I need to really take care things like shaving my legs.

So, I pamper and preen as best I can, rapidly shaving my legs and slathering on lotion, then choosing my nicest pair of jeans and a snug-fitting pale green sweater. My thick hair will take forever to dry, and I have hardly any makeup, so I'll have to do my best. Feeling a bit guilty, I sneak into Bailey's room and borrow some lip gloss, mentally promising myself I'll get her new stuff when I get paid.

Shit. I have like one minute left.

I grab a light jacket and my bag, then race out the door, ignoring the smell of cigarettes and pot that lingers in the hallway. I smile to myself when I see the gleaming car out front, and suddenly remember he said he'd have the money wired to my account this morning. *Yes. God, yes.* My throat feels tight and my nose tingles. I could get money in a lot of other ways, and maybe I'm betraying myself a little with this. But I'm not going to think about it. Not now.

Manuel stands beside the door of the car and bows his head to me.

"Good morning, miss," he says.

"Glad you didn't call me ma'am," I say. "Or we'd have to have words."

His eyes crinkle around the edges with a smile as he opens the door. "Yes, ma'am."

"Manuel," I say with a huff. "Do I have to speak to Mr. Alexander about this?"

To my utter shock, he immediately sobers and shakes his head. "No, Miss Myers," he says. "My apologies."

I feel ashamed of myself, as if I'm abusing some

kind of authority I didn't even know I had. Good God, what kind of power does Liam yield?

"No worries," I say, feeling like a total fake. I'm just a college girl wearing borrowed lip gloss and thrift store clothes, climbing into this expensive car and wielding power that isn't mine. But before I can say another thing, the door closes and I'm in the luxurious leather interior. I pinch the bridge of my nose to get my shit together, and my stomach churns. I haven't had anything to eat, which is probably just as well. It would be nice if I lost a few pounds if he's going to see me naked again.

If?

Then I remember how he sat me on his knee and gave me a warning smack for talking badly about my body.

Maybe... maybe he likes me just the way I am. I don't quite get it, but it's a weird concept.

I'm so used to thinking of myself as a work in progress.

If only I could lose some weight. If only I could take the time to be well-rested and eat well. If only I had my degree. If only...

I square my shoulders. Today, I have a job to do, and when I put my mind to something, I do it well. The car cruises to a stop outside a high-rise with gleaming mirrored windows that go so far up, I have to crane my neck to see.

"We've arrived, Miss Myers."

TWELVE

Liam

I GLANCE at my watch and tap a button to Manuel.

"Was she on time?" I ask.

"Yes, sir, Mr. Alexander," he says.

"Good." Punctuality matters to me, and I've got a lot to cover before Manuel brings her to class.

I answer four emails before I hear a knock on the door. "Come in," I say, distracted.

"Ms. Myers is here to see you, sir," Mandy says, opening the door and ushering Cora in.

"Have a seat, Ms. Myers," I say, not even looking her way. Mandy shuts the door, as she knows I don't like to be interrupted when I'm working. Scowling at the screen, I discard three emails of no consequence and check my agenda. Then I turn to Cora.

"Good morning, Mr. Alexander," she says politely, but there's a hardness to her jaw and glint in her eyes that I already know to be a warning.

"Good morning, Ms. Myers," I say. Formalities it is.

There are so many things I want to do to her. So many things I want to say. We need this contract signed as soon as possible.

Jake had the contract ready on my desk before I arrived at work, with a post-it note scribbled on the top.

"You are aware this is the girl who's trying to undermine your project?"

I tear the note up and trash it. I couldn't give two shits about her little social justice project. I'll continue with my plans, and what happens on school grounds stays on school grounds.

"Please step into the restroom for a minute?" I tell her. "The instructions are in there as to the tests you'll take."

"Oh, lovely," she mutters. "Just so you know, I've had sex twice in my life and both times the guys were virgins, so the chances of me having a damn STD are slim and none."

I smirk at my computer screen and nod. "Noted." I've paid for expedited testing, so we'll have the results before lunchtime. A few minutes later, she comes back into my office.

"Please review the terms of your contract," I tell her coolly. Ignoring the way her hair smells, still damp from the shower, I immediately go back to the night before, then push the memory out of my mind. We have a job to do before we play again.

Clicking the pen I hand her, she captures her full lower lip between her teeth and studies the contract.

"Question," she says. "Please clarify the terms of when and where I'm obligated to abide by these rules." A lock of red hair falls across her brow when she quirks a brow at me. Hastily she swipes it away, and I want to be the one tucking it behind her ear.

Jesus, I've got to get a grip.

"I've given that some thought," I tell her sternly. I want her listening. "My preference would be all the time."

She blinks at me. "So... a total power exchange? I thought this was more of a part-time thing..."

"You've done your research," I say with a smile. "Not a total power exchange. I won't be able to control what you do when you're at school or at home," I say, "though I will have my methods."

The familiar faint pink colors her cheeks. "Okay. And I am allowed to safeword when I want to. Yes?"

"Yes, of course," I say. I clench my jaw. We've already discussed this. I insist on safewords but dislike the thought of her using one.

Nodding, she places her pen at the line at the

bottom of the page. "I think this will be a challenge," she says, smiling. "And honestly, Liam... um, sir?"

I nod.

She grins. "I kinda like a challenge."

She hasn't signed yet, though. She's giving it another read.

"As do I," I say, but I'm not amused. We'll see how much of a challenge she really likes. "Tonight, I'll pick you up and we'll go to Verge. We have a few matters of business to discuss."

"We do," she says. "Yes."

"First, your phone." I take the slim white box out of the desk drawer where I put it this morning, and hand it to her. "Learn it. My number's programmed on it, and I've had my man sync it to your old one."

"How'd you do that?" she asks, adorably bemused, her lips pressed together.

"It wasn't hard, Cora. We contacted your cell phone company and paid them for their time. So, you should find your old apps restored, with two additions. My contact information and I've installed a tracking app that will tell me where you are at all times."

"Isn't that a violation of privacy?"

I shrug. "We have our methods."

"Great," she says. "I mean, I needed a phone and want it synced, I just don't like you going through my things."

I turn back to my computer and minimize my email. My phone lights up like a runway with the calls I've got waiting for me.

"Do I look like I have the time to go through your cell phone?" I ask with a shake of my head. "I have no interest."

"Well," she murmurs. "Alright then. Okay. So. Let me take a look."

"You'll learn to say please and not issue commands to me."

She takes a deep breath. "Please?" Scowling, she gives me minimal obedience.

I wonder how long she can keep that scowl in place when my belt meets her ass.

She looks at the contract and reads it through again. "Item six is silly, you know," she says. "I didn't think you were serious when you said it."

"I was dead serious," I told her. "I've done this enough times to know what we're doing is dangerous. Emotions, vulnerability, and trust are gateways for things neither of us wish." I ignore the way she flinches.

"For God's sake, you can be an arrogant prick," she says, then quickly clamps a hand to her mouth. "Oh. Um. Sorry?" she whispers. "Does that get me punished?"

I lean back in my chair and hold her gaze with mine. "After the contract? You'd feel my belt for that, sweetheart." And hell, I mean it. My dick throbs at the thought of the first time she mouths off to me when I'm allowed to punish her. Disciplining a mouthy little thing like her is fucking rewarding.

Swallowing, she looks out the window. "So... you can say whatever you want, and I'm supposed to just take it? Is that fair?"

"There's nothing fair about a power exchange," I tell her. "You're signing an *agreement* for there to be an imbalance of power."

"But... but wait," she says, crossing her arms on her chest. Her eyes are bright, her cheeks flushed. Hell, I love it when she gets all fired up like this.

"Yes?"

"It is fair, though," she says. "When a... couple... engages in the power exchange. It shouldn't be one sided. Yes, the submissive partner agrees to... abide by the rules," she says, turning pink and waving at the papers on my desk. I know now the blush of her cheeks isn't always nerves, but passion. Christ, I love that. "But there's a payoff, and I don't mean financial."

I didn't expect this from her, to be honest. But hell, she's right. I just wasn't prepared to get into this.

"There is," I tell her. "And there will be a payoff. When you agree to this contract, there's far more than money that will make it worth your time. Frankly, Cora, if I wanted nothing more than paid sex, I'd hire a prostitute."

I love when her eyes flash at me, but I ignore her silent outrage and continue.

"I *like* being the one in charge. And yes, sweetheart. You'll glean more than a well-filled bank account." I glance at my watch. "And we can discuss this at length when we have more time. You have twenty minutes before you need to leave for class. Are you going to sign the contract or what?"

I watch as her eyes go from the papers to the pen in her hand, to the phone, and back to the papers again. She's warring with herself, and I'm glad that she is. That she's taking this seriously. It's no small request I've made of her, and I'll be pushing her damn hard against her limits.

Inhaling so deeply her shoulders rise, she lifts her chin and gives me a curt nod. "Yes. I told you I would, and I always do what I say I will." Grasping the pen in hand, she signs her name on the space provided with a flourish, then hands the pen to me. I look at the contract one final time. Glance over the curvy, embellished signature, then sign my own name below it. My signature below hers, all slashes and angles, is in such contrast to her loops and swirls.

A thrill runs through me.

She's mine.

All fucking mine.

I stand, watching her body tighten as I leave my desk like she thinks I'm approaching but I'm not. I know exactly what I have in mind. I walk past her, head to the door, and flick the lock. My team knows me well. My door flashes a red *occupied* sign on the other side of the door when I lock it. They know not to trouble me with anything unless it's a life or death situation. When the lock clicks into place with an audible snap, Cora jumps.

"Come here." I stand in front of the door and beckon, energy crackling through me like fire, dynamic and dangerous. Consuming. My first instruction to her as my submissive. Monumental in its simplicity.

Almost poetic.

Come, where danger and eroticism meld, folding together in a seamless garment of pleasure and pain.

Come and lay your will at my feet.

Come to the threshold of ecstasy.

Come hard and often and without inhibition.

Rising, she shoots me an apprehensive glance laced with eagerness and fear. I point to the floor and assume the tone she knows to obey.

"On your knees, sweetheart."

We have no time to fully enter into the dance of power play, but I can prime her for this evening.

Blinking, she drops to her knees uncertainly, caution in those mesmerizing depths.

I crook my finger at her. A silent command.

Prowling toward me like a lioness, her eyes never leave mine. I drop to one knee and wait for her. Every inch she closes between us makes my heart race faster, until she's so close I can feel the vibration of her breath.

"Good girl," I whisper, taking her hands so she kneels in front of me, I gently arrange them behind her back so that she arches, her full breasts nearly brushing my chest. "This is one of many ways you'll present yourself to me. I will teach you, and we will practice. On your knees."

"Hands clasped behind your back." I trace my palms from her shoulders to her folded hands and clasp mine over hers.

"Head bowed down." I grasp her chin between my thumb and forefinger and bend her head down, loving the way the light illuminates the vibrant hair that falls down in sheets of brilliance. I allow myself the briefest of touches, running my hand from the top of her head to the base of her neck. Smooth as satin, fragrant and beautiful, still slightly damp from her early morning shower.

"Knees spread apart." Gently, I nudge her knees apart with the tips of my fingers. "You'll hold this position whenever I give the command to kneel. Do you understand me?"

I lift her chin with my knuckle, raising her eyes to mine, and when she nods, I lower my mouth to hers, just the whisper of a kiss before I pull away.

I'll leave her wanting.

Standing, I take her hand in mine and tug so that she gets to her feet, a full head shorter than I am.

"You leave in minutes," I tell her. "Later tonight, we'll pick up where we started. Strip."

She's obeyed so well, I'm a bit surprised by her hesitation, but when she doesn't obey, I smack her ass on instinct. It's all she needs, before she quickly begins to undress. There's question in her eyes, but I have no time to ease her into this. When her clothes lie in a puddle on the floor, I take her by the hand and lead her to the small room off of my main office. I have to look away; she's so beautiful and we don't have time for the ways I want to worship that body of hers.

We will.

Here, in the walk-in closet I've had built beside the bathroom and workout area, her clothes await.

"You'll dress in what I give you to wear," I tell her. "This is your outfit for today."

"I... will you... am I allowed to speak?"

"Of course," I tell her. "Unless I've given you the instruction not to. But I haven't yet, so you may."

"Will you dress me every day? Like I'll have to come here before anything or... whatever?"

"It depends on the day," I tell her. "Within a few weeks your old clothes will be put away and you'll only have what I've given you." I take a silky pair of pink panties from the small pile I've prepared, bend, and help her step into them. They hug her curves beautifully. Next, I help her slide on a matching bra. She's going to school, so I've chosen a simple outfit for today, slim-fitting black leggings with a soft, clingy hunter-green top, and knee-high boots.

"Oh, wow," she says when she's dressed. "These are kind of amazing."

Manuel's ringtone sounds at my desk. He's ready to take her to class.

"*You're* kind of amazing," I say, tugging her

head back and giving her a quick kiss. "Tonight, I'll take you to Verge. When your class is over, Manuel will bring you back to me. I will text you instructions to follow throughout the day, and you'll report to me when you come back. Understand?"

"Yes, sir," she says, nodding, and a little smile plays at her lips like she can't quite grasp what we're doing. "Are you going to make it impossible for me to focus? I mean, I have school..."

"Of course, you do," I tell her. "But you're a smart girl. I'm sure you'll manage just fine. But one more thing before you go."

"Oh?"

"Every day when we part, I'll leave you with a reminder of our agreement," I tell her. "So that no matter how you're otherwise preoccupied, you will remember your place."

"A reminder?" she asks, a note of confusion in her voice.

"Some days, it'll be a small, visceral memento." I remove the pen I slipped into my pocket and place my hand out, palm up, for her hand. When she lays her hand in mine, I draw a tiny heart at the vee between her thumb and index finger. "I want to see that tonight when I meet you at Verge. Understood?"

"Yes, sir," she says, staring with a furrowed brow at her hand.

Usually I need to apply some punishment to a new submissive before she remembers to address me properly, but Cora's taken to this well.

"And other times, the memento will be...?" her voice trails off as she waits for me to supply an answer. I won't, though.

"You'll see," is all she gets from me. "Now go to class."

I escort her to where Manuel waits, and go back to my work. A little while later, my phone buzzes.

Checking in, sir. I'm at class. Attached to the text is a picture of her hand resting on her notebook, the little black heart at the epicenter.

Good girl. She'll be rewarded tonight for a job well done.

The morning passes quickly, and when I break for lunch, Jake arrives looking cross. "Come in," I tell him, irritated he's up my ass like this.

"They're causing trouble again, Liam," he says, mopping his perpetually ruddy forehead with a handkerchief.

"Who?" I ask, turning away from him.

"The damn college students. Namely, the girl."

I want to deck his smug, pug-like face, but I school my features. He knows I've just entered into a contract with one of those "damn college students."

"So?" I ask him. "Your point? The social justice warriors love to give me shit. Since when did that become an issue?"

I turn back to my computer and answer the emails that wait for me when my phone vibrates with a message from Cora. I pick up my phone and read her reply.

Heard and obeyed, sir.

I swallow hard and almost forget Jake's sitting in front of me. She was instructed to find a vacant bathroom and send me a sexy text. I turn my phone face-down before Jake sees it.

"...and if we don't do something about this, they could ruin you."

I snort with ridicule. "Jake, that's bullshit. Stop wasting my time."

"You seem totally unruffled," he responds, irritated with me. "Does this mean nothing to you?"

"I pay you to be *ruffled* for me," I tell him. "So, unless you have something of real importance to tell me, you can leave now. I have work to do before I leave."

I'm half paying attention to the way his cheeks flame with indignation, before he gathers up his papers and leaves the room. This is utter bullshit. I shake my head and mindlessly eat my lunch, but nearly drop my phone and groan when I get a text from Cora.

A picture.

It isn't the cleavage shot I expect, or something more lascivious, but a close up of her lips. She's got her lower lip captured between her teeth, and her head bowed in submission.

Jesus, it's so beautiful I want to hire a painter to capture that pose so I can hold it forever.

That's it, beautiful. Just what I like to see. You've earned yourself a good girl spanking for that.

There's a lengthy pause before she responds.

I... have no idea what that means, sir.

I smile.

I'll show you.

THIRTEEN

Cora

GOOD GIRL SPANKING.

It seems like a fairly counterintuitive concept. I mean, spankings are for bad girls. Punishment. But as I finish up my classes, I find myself growing hotter, squirming with the vision of being draped over Liam's lap. I'm so turned on by the way he's played with me today, the friction between my legs when I walk makes heat thrum through my core.

God, I'm out of control, like my sex drive is on hyper alert.

How did this even happen? I'm just a plain girl with a snarky mouth and curves that go on for days. I pause smack dab in the middle of the campus and try to turn around to look at my ass. What does he see in me? By most people's standards, I tip the scale toward chubby—

I feel my mind come to a screeching halt. Jesus. He's not even here, but I can hear him chide me.

If you were mine, I'd turn you over my knee for a comment like that.

He said that once. Am I his now?

My signature on that document says I sure as hell am.

I'm glad that my classes today were easy, because I was way more intent on the kinky pleasure and pain that awaits me than I was on any lectures I heard. I don't really know what a good girl spanking is, but it sounds like a reward. One I'm seriously dying to earn.

I glance at the time as I finish my last class. I have just enough time to get home for Bailey and Ben, give them a super quick run-down of what's going on—um, I have a new job or something—get them fed, and wait for Liam's ride to Verge.

I wish I had a bookstore shift today, but I only work there when my classes end at noon. Maybe Chandra or Marla will be at Verge tonight?

I take my new shiny phone and hold it like its dynamite. I'm not used to uber expensive things like this. It's small but slick, and so fast it's like it does what I want it to before I even touch the screen. Crazy. Will this go away when our contract is up?

Damn. Re-entry will be hard.

But then I remind myself of the money he

wired into my account today, and my heart races. God, I want this so badly.

"Cora?" I turn to see Giada approaching me.

"Hey," I say, smiling at her. I haven't seen her in a while, and we greet each other with a brief hug. "I thought you were done taking classes?"

"I am," she says. "But I actually came to meet a..." her voice trails off and she shoots me a secret little smile... "friend of mine for lunch."

It's still a well-kept secret on campus that Giada dates Geoffrey, a professor of literature here. She's no longer a student, but she sure as hell was when they met, so we all keep it a little quiet.

"Ah, nice."

"I saw your name on a protest sign at the bookstore," she asks, tipping her head to the side. "Are you on a crusade?"

"Yep," I tell her, but suddenly I don't feel so good about this anymore. I don't want to think of Liam the businessman, because that one's an asshole. I prefer Liam the dom.

Both, sweetheart. I'm both.

"What's it all about?" she asks. God, I wish I could tell her everything. I could seriously use some advice, and Liam doesn't have any clauses in our contract that prohibit me from talking to anyone. Still, discretion is best, and we both know that.

"Well... the Greenery is under construction," I tell her. It saddens me a little that the cause that meant so much to me even a week ago seems so silly now. People are starving to death in third world countries, boys and girls who aren't old enough to drink are enlisting in the army and willing to put their lives on the line, women and children are being abused and mistreated... and I'm concerned about The Greenery?

Well, yes. Yes, I am.

"Is it?" she asks. "Wow. Well that sucks. And you're protesting to try to prevent it?"

"Yeah," I say, and it sounds a little hollow.

"Nice," she says with conviction. "I'm proud of you. See you at the club tonight?"

I breathe a sigh of relief, because I don't want to talk about this anymore, and I like feeling like I belong at Verge.

"Yeah," I tell her. "I'm, um, not tending bar anymore, though."

Giada gives me a bold wink. "I know, babe. And all I've gotta say is *good for you!*" Leaning in, she gives me a quick hug, the fragrance of her perfume reminding me how very different we are. Giada is the one who should be in my position, not little ol' me. She's thin and beautiful and elegant, walking away from me on those heels I'd kill myself on. No wonder Geoff fairly worships the ground she walks in.

I sigh.

I suck at this, and I'm not super happy about the reminder of my damn crusade that Liam's going to raze with the blink of an eye.

My phone vibrates with a text from him.

Tests are all clear. You're mine.

My heart stutters in my chest and my mouth goes dry. Oh, boy. So now sex is on the table, too, apparently.

I walk home in a daze, completely forgetting that Liam told me I'm supposed to get a ride from Manuel, and I'm about a block away when my phone rings.

When I see Liam on the caller I.D. I suddenly remember.

Shit.

"Hello?"

"Hello *what?*" he bites.

I look around me, and we're in NYC so of course there are a million people in every direction. Whatever.

"Hello, sir," I say. What crawled up his ass?

"Where the hell are you?"

"I'm walking home," I tell him. "I'm at the corner of Rose and Trinket Ave. And shouldn't you know, since you've got the tracking app?"

"Yeah, but I wanted to hear you say it. Stay right there. Do not fucking move."

Click.

Well. I guess he takes this sort of seriously.

He's gone, and I'm standing in the middle of the sidewalk being jostled by people who walk by. My heart trips an erratic beat in my chest. Damn, I suck at this. I mentally berate myself until I see the familiar black car cruising to a stop beside me. The door opens, and Liam steps out, walks over to me, takes me by the arm, and hauls me into the car.

I sit quickly and reach for my seatbelt, but he's already got it in hand. Buckling me in with a scowl, he finally sits back and shoots me a fierce look of reproval.

"I forgot," I say with a shrug.

"Right," he says. "I'll be happy to remind you tonight."

"Oh?" I ask, my heartbeat racing. "Um. What might that entail?"

Not blinking, his eyes blaze into mine. "Six with the cane should do it."

I look down, chastened. Jesus. A cane? Of course, I've never had it before, but he's the one in charge and I agreed to it.

"Well. Okay," I say. "I'm sorry. But you know it's going to take time getting used to this, right?" I hazard a glance back up at him, and see his gaze begin to soften. "I've never had a driver before."

Sighing, he takes my hand in his. "Yeah, Cora," he says. "I'm sorry. I overreacted. I didn't see you where we were supposed to meet, and I thought the worst. I tried calling you, but it went to voicemail. You must've been in a dead zone or something."

"It didn't even ring," I tell him, and even though I feel his reproval, my heart does a little somersault.

He cares.

God, he *cares*.

And literally no one ever has before.

Hell, I love that.

"So... does your overreaction mean no, um,

cane?" I ask. Oh my God I don't even like saying the word.

I may be imagining it, but his eyes twinkle a bit even as he frowns at me. And then his voice softens, which does unpredictable things to my body. "I don't think so."

I feel like I'm going to cry when he says in a soft voice, "I just don't want to see you hurt, Cora. Now give me a kiss and make me forget I need to cane you later."

I actually smile when he leans in to greet me with a kiss.

The car cruises to a stop. "So... you know I need to run upstairs and check on them, right?"

"I do," he says. "Thirty minutes enough time?"

"Yes," I tell him.

"Just so we're clear, I'd prefer to be going up with you," he says with a scowl that I swear is almost a pout, "but I know you want a little privacy. But you keep your phone in your hand while you walk and if I text, you answer immediately. Got it?"

"Yes, sir."

He's already pulling out his phone and opening his email when I open the door. I want to be quick about it.

I exit the car and head toward the entrance to my building.

"Cora. There you are."

I inwardly groan. Is this "bump into Cora on the street" day?

"Yes?"

It's my landlord at the entryway to the building, holding a cigarette between her dry, cracked lips and peering at me through dirty glasses. "Rent, or street? This is getting old."

I brush past her. "I'll have a check in your mailbox within the hour."

"That's what they all say," she says, reaching for my arm, her nails biting into me. I try to tug away, but she's got a firm grip.

"Let me go," I tell her. I could pull away, but this is complicated. If I hurt my landlord... "I promise—"

"Is there a problem here?" We both freeze.

I almost forgot how tall Liam is until he's towering over the tiny woman who cowers in his wake. She lets me go like I'm on fire and stares up at him with wide-eyes and her mouth parted in a perfect "O." Though he's shrugged out of his suit coat and removed his tie, he looks every bit the part of someone who so does *not* belong standing outside an apartment building like mine.

And he's with *me*.

I barely refrain from sticking my tongue out at her like a child, but I'm victorious. He got out of the car to defend me, and I've never had someone stand up for me like this.

I like it.

"No, there's no problem," she says, her eyes going from me to him and back again, then roving the expensive cut of his suit. "She your girlfriend?"

"It's none of your business who he is," I snap,

saving him from having to answer, but her shrewd little eyes take in the new phone in my hand and the nice clothes that I'm wearing.

"Isn't it?" she asks.

"You said there was no problem," Liam reminds her, giving me a gentle push to the door. "We need to go."

"You know," I say, keeping my gaze fixed on her. "Why don't you come up with me after all?'

It surprises me how much I like watching his eyes light up like that, like I've just granted him something that makes him happy, but as soon as he starts to come with me, I regret my momentary lack of discretion.

I don't want him here. How will I explain his presence to Bailey and Ben?

He's too good for a place like this.

But as we make our way in the apartment building, he's talking about the landlord and holding my elbow, and I suddenly don't care about our threadbare couch but wonder what Ben and Bailey will think. Hell, I need them to meet him, though. I'm his for the next two months.

"...and if she ever puts her hands on you again, Cora, you call the police. I mean it. Do you understand me?"

"Yes, of course," I tell him. "I promise. I was... a little late with the rent this month, but that will be taken care of now."

Stopping on a landing, he pulls me to him and fixes me with a steady look that borders on a glare.

"That *doesn't* give her the right to physically intimidate you."

"Only you get to do that?" I ask before I can stop myself.

And then his mouth is on mine, and it doesn't matter that the light in the hall is dim and covered in cobwebs or that some kind of rap music blares so loudly down the hall the balls of my feet are vibrating, or that it smells faintly like burnt microwaved popcorn and curry. None of that matters, because all I see is the blue of his eyes. All I hear is the pounding of my heart. All I smell is Liam, the brisk musk of his cologne, both soothing and classy, and everything else fades.

Every time he kisses me, a little part of me draws closer to him.

Every time he kisses me, I lose a little of the stronghold I have on my emotions.

Every time he kisses me, I'm more in danger of breaking rule number six *and that cannot happen.*

I pull away too soon, because I can't let Bailey or Ben see us. Not like this.

"I need to get my things," I say, pulling away too soon and not letting myself look into those eyes for one more second. I take out my keys and face the door.

"I... I have to admit, I wish I hadn't invited you up here," I tell him. "Please keep in mind our place is very... *simple.*" My hands are shaking so badly I can't fit the key in the lock. I turn my back to him so he doesn't see, but it doesn't matter. His hand dwarfs mine, steadying my trembling fingers, and he glides the key in the lock but doesn't turn it quite yet.

"I didn't come here to look at your apartment or eat a gourmet meal," he tells me. "I came here because you're mine for the next two months, and I keep what's mine safe."

I don't know how I feel about what he said. I like that he came up with me. I like that he's calling me his. I shouldn't, but I do.

But... I'm only his by contract, so that makes this act of chivalry really for his benefit.

Or something.

I think.

Doesn't it?

He pushes the door open before I can sort my thoughts. Bailey's laying on the couch, ear buds in, singing her heart out, and Ben is sitting at the dining room table with the same Lego set he's been building and reconstructing for six months. He freezes when we walk in, his large eyes rounded in surprise at the sight of Liam.

I don't blame him. Not only is Liam dressed for the office, he's huge and intimidating, taking up the whole doorway.

"Hi," I say, and Bailey still doesn't realize I'm home, as her eyes are closed while she's crooning to the music. "Um, Bailey?" I say, casting a sideways glance to Liam. His lips twitch, but he tucks his hands in his pocket and steps inside the door, trying to be as unobtrusive as he can, which is honestly not super effective. Shutting the door, he checks the lock, then frowns when he realizes there's no dead-bolt. I don't miss the disproving look he shoots me. I shrug. Something tells me we'll be talking about that later.

Why do I like how ridiculously overprotective he is? How he gets angry at the thought of my safety? I don't mean anything to him. This is really nothing but a front.

"Hi," Ben says. "Wow. Who are you?"

Liam reaches his hand out to shake Ben's. "Liam," he says. "And you're Ben?"

Bailey chooses that moment to open her eyes, and her reaction would be comical if I wasn't so on edge. She squeals and tries to sit up, but in her excitement, she topples sideways off the couch and falls to the floor on hands and knees.

Ben snorts with laughter and Liam starts coughing, which sounds suspiciously like he's trying to cover up a laugh himself.

"Um, hi, guys," I say. Bailey tries to get to her feet gracefully, but her earbuds are wrapped around her ear and her hair's askew, and the poor thing's bright red in the face.

"Hi," she manages weakly. I motion for her to take her ear buds out, and she scrambles to do it, her cheeks flushing.

"So, um. This is Liam," I say. And to my relief, Liam isn't looking at the worn sofa and thin walls, the carpet that's so old and worn it's little more than tatters, the cheap linoleum floor in the kitchen or the bare lightbulb that hangs from the ceiling. He's reaching a hand out to Bailey and giving her the warmest smile I've ever seen from him.

I didn't know he could smile like that, with his eyes crinkling around the edges and his mouth crooked and charming.

Jesus, I wish I still didn't know he could smile like that.

"What are you guys doing here?" Bailey asks, trying to get herself together.

"We have, um..." How do I say it? *I have to fulfill my contract as a high-end prostitute tonight.* "I wanted to come see you before I have to go to work tonight." I can't look her in her eyes. I don't want her to know what exactly that work entails. "How did things go today?"

Ben tells me about his science project for the fair next week and runs to his room to get it. Liam takes a seat at the very edge of our couch. He's so big in comparison to the dilapidated thing that he looks as if he's going to fall straight to the floor, but it doesn't seem to bother him.

Where is the aloof, cool demeanor? Where's the scorn and anger I've come to expect? This guy seems almost... *nice.*

"It was a good day," Bailey says. "I got my first 'A' in geometry, but don't get your hopes up because I'm sure it was a total fluke," she mutters.

"God, geometry," Liam mutters, shaking his head. Bailey flushes beet red.

"Good job," I tell her. I look back to Liam. "Um, is what I'm wearing okay for tonight?"

"Why wouldn't it be okay to tend bar?" Bailey asks, confused.

Liam smiles. "Fine, Cora," and somehow the deep, steady timbre of his voice settles my fraught nerves, but I can read that wolfish grin of his.

It doesn't matter what you wear. It's coming off.

Ben comes back into the room with a contraption I haven't seen before, with a penny and wires and a potato and lightbulb. I have some vague recollection of a similar science experiment in my grade school years, but I know nothing about Ben doing a project, and a little part of me is sad that I didn't even help him with this. I look to Bailey, who notes the question in my eyes and nods. She helped him with it and hell, I didn't even know he was doing it. I swallow back the tears that threaten to blur my vision.

I can't help this. I'm not out partying with friends and neglecting my brother and sister. Hell, I'm barely taking care of myself. I'm trying to keep us together with what little I've got, trying to keep us from falling apart.

I have to.

I walk to the kitchen to cook them some food, opening the cabinets, when Bailey reminds me, "Hey, um, remember you said you were ordering pizza tonight?" When Liam looks up at her she flushes nearly purple, puts her head down, and joins me in the kitchen.

"Oh, right. Pizza," I said.

"You can't let Ben down. He's been dying for *real* pizza," she says.

"Of course not," I say. I pick up my phone, but I'm flustered, and my fingers won't work quite right. I'm not really sure why. It isn't just Liam sitting in this room, and my fraught nerves at letting him down. It isn't just the run-in with my landlady, or the discussion with Giada, or all the unanswered questions Bailey will have for me that I don't really know the answer to. It isn't the essay I need written by Friday or the exam coming up. Or hell, the punishment I've got coming tonight at Verge, and whatever Liam decides to do to me when he has me alone.

It's everything.

"But it doesn't exactly work the way it's supposed to," Ben is saying, frowning. "And I don't really know why."

"I know why," Liam says, but instead of taking it out of Ben's hands and fixing it, he looks at Ben and asks politely, "May I show you?"

Ben's eyes light up.

"Just let me order the pizza first, okay?" Liam asks.

I swallow hard.

Don't be nice to them. Please, don't be nice to them.

"Cora," Bailey whispers. "Who is this guy? What the hell have you been hiding from me?"

Liam asks Ben what kind of pizza he likes, and

Bailey and I give him our requests. When he puts the phone up to his ear to order, Bailey hisses in my ear.

"Where the *hell* did you find that god of a man, who is he, and, *I repeat,* what exactly are you hiding from me?"

"*Bailey,*" I hiss back. It's so not cool my kid sister's calling him a *god of a man.*

"*Cora,*" she responds.

Jesus.

"His name is Liam," I tell her, which only earns me an eye roll and she smacks my arm playfully.

"I got that part, sis."

"I met him at the coffee shop," I tell her in a whisper. "And we're sort of dating."

"Sort of?" She gives me an *I wasn't born yesterday* kinda look.

"Okay, so I'm not really sure what we're doing."

"Hmm," she says with an exaggerated tap to her chin. "Is there *smooching*?"

"Smooching?" I snort, getting the attention of both Liam *and* Ben. I shoot them my most winsome, *nothing to see here, folks* smile and give her a shrug. "Well a little."

"*God,*" she whispers. "And um... gotta say. I'm not like super experienced in this area, but that man does *not* look like he uses drugstore aftershave and takes a cab to work. He looks like he belongs on the cover of *GQ* or something."

"Damnit, I know," I say on a groan. But Liam's hanging up the phone and turning back to Ben.

Bailey's eyes shoot from me to him and back to me, then she picks up her phone and gives me a pointed look so obvious it's almost comical.

My phone buzzes with a text from her. I roll my eyes.

Friends with benefits? Did you sleep with him???

I huff out in indignation and text her back. *I did not and stop asking details of my sex life. When the hell would I have time to sleep with him?*

But it's a flimsy excuse and I can't even look at her because hell, *I know*. I'm gonna sleep with him.

Methinks the lady doth protest too much.

My mouth falls open in shock and I shoot her a glare, but her lips are pressed in a thin line and she's shaking her head from side to side. I want to smack some sense into the girl with her Shakespearean clichés.

You think too much about sex, I shoot back in reply, giving her what I hope is an effective older-sister glare.

Fine, she texts, and sighs dramatically.

He IS rich, though, right?

Well, yeah. And this conversation is SO over.

I plunk my phone down on the counter to end this conversation, but the little instigator gives me a once-over as if she's just noticing my clothes.

"Nice clothes," she says in a whisper. "And a new phone? Girl, you are *so* holding out on me."

I sigh. There's no use denying it any longer. I won't lie to her, she certainly isn't going to get the whole truth, but I can at least give her as much as I can.

"We met, and I'm sort of seeing him," I tell her. "But he isn't *really* a boyfriend. I hardly know him, honey. So. Let's take a look at that geometry," I tell her. "I have to go really soon, and I can do my best to help you first."

Looking across the room, she suddenly realizes she needs to cross in front of Liam to get her book. I shake my head and roll my eyes and go get her book.

Ben hoots and pumps his fist into the air, and I sneak a glance over at them. Liam's got the penny at an angle, pointing to something, and the light-bulb is actually lit up.

I'm not used to him being like this, all normal nice guy, instead of the sadistic millionaire who drew a heart on my hand today and will likely find far more intrusive methods of "giving me a memento" in the future. And I don't trust Mr. Nice Guy. I'm more used to the man I'm supposed to hate.

I do my best with Bailey's math, but we're struggling with one problem when Liam joins us at the counter. "Don't forget that a negative times a negative equals a positive," he says, pointing at a mark on the paper.

"Oh, right," I say. We fix the problem, but I freeze when he bends down and plants the briefest but chaste kiss on my forehead just as the bell rings.

"Not a boyfriend," Bailey says in a hissed

whisper and an exaggerated eye roll when Liam goes to get the door. "Because friends totally look at you like that and *kiss your forehead.* And *look at you like that.*"

"Stop it or I'll tell him you said that," I threaten, using the only warning I know will work.

Her huge eyes go from me to him and she clamps her mouth shut.

I tell myself her foolish notions have seriously gone to her head, but I want to know what way he looks at me.

No, I don't.

Yes, I do.

Fucking. Rule. Number. Six.

We eat pizza and laugh at Ben's story about the Wildlife team that visited his school today and how the mouse got away from the instructor and chaos erupted in the classroom. This is easy and comfortable, and I don't like that it is. He's charming them, damnit. This isn't our normal, and I don't care about *me,* but I don't like the idea of Ben and Bailey getting attached to a guy who won't be here in a few months. I don't like it at all.

So, when we're done eating, I stand and wipe my hands on a napkin. "We need to get going, guys," I tell them. I can feel the irritation building. How dare he come in here and beguile them like this? "You all set for tonight?"

Liam stands to the side, giving me space to handle getting them settled. Finally, we leave, after

I whisper into Bailey's ear that I'll fill her in with *some* details later.

I can't get out of there fast enough.

No more getting attached to Liam.

Am I telling myself for their sake or mine?

FOURTEEN

Liam

"WELL, you didn't have to go and charm their socks off," Cora snaps when we reach the stairs.

"Wait. What?" I ask her. That was the most normal visit I've paid to anyone in years. Hell, I enjoyed myself, and now she's going to turn this around? Oh no, she doesn't. I have no patience for this bullshit, and she needs to listen to me now. "That's enough, Cora. We'll talk in the car."

"I don't—"

Out of patience, I give her a silent swat to the rear that silences her and makes her cheeks color pink.

Manuel's waiting for us and opens the door when we arrive. I help her in, then step into the car behind her, shut the door and wait until we pull away from the curb before I speak.

"There's no need to chide me," I tell her. "I went upstairs with you because you were accosted by that bitch, and I visited with your brother and sister. We ate dinner and did homework. What's so wrong with that?"

"What's *wrong* with that?" she sputters, and I can tell by the way her voice goes high-pitched and her eyes are too bright that she's really, truly upset. I'm confused and getting angry at the way she's looking at me, like I did something wrong. Hell, I'm used to pissing her off when her anger's justified, but this is ridiculous.

"What's *wrong* with that?" she repeats. "They don't need you swooping in here all gallant and heroic and growing attached to you like you're some sort of filthy rich fairy godmother—no, sugar daddy—*brother* or *whatever-the-fuck.* You can't solve everything with your money, you know. There are some things that money can't buy, and the hearts of children who've experienced far more devastation and heartache than children *ever should* are one of them!"

I don't know if I'm angry or surprised or both. I don't know if I want to kiss those pouty lips of hers to silence her or take her across my knee for mouthing off and teach her to speak to her dom with respect.

"Excuse me? What the actual *fuck* are you talking about? I ordered pizza."

"Oh, let me show you how to do that science experiment," she mocks. "What kind of pizza do you like?" she flings at me. "Why don't I—"

Now I've truly had enough of this. "Jesus, woman. This is bullshit. You're making way too big a deal out of this."

"What's bullshit?" she tosses back at me. "I'm not playing, Liam. I never should have—"

It's taking considerable effort not to raise my voice.

"That's. Enough." She freezes and looks at me with wide eyes, as if suddenly realizing she's crossed a line. "You listen to me. I don't care if you're insecure about where you live or who you are, and you're worried about your siblings. I went in there with literally no hidden agenda and actually fucking *enjoyed* my visit with Bailey and Ben until you flew off the handle."

She blinks. "You did?"

"I did. I have no siblings. I grew up raised by nannies and in boarding schools with more money than I knew what to do with. I had horses when I was younger and cars when I was older, and a legacy to uphold. You may have been dealt a shit hand in life, but you know what? There are many types of poverty, Cora."

This time, she says nothing, but she pales a little and seems to shrink in her seat. I've got a point to make, and hell, this girl is gonna listen.

"I may have had money, but I had no parents to care for me. I was an arrogant prick who had no friends, and no skills to obtain any. I've never had a romantic relationship of any kind, since the only types of interaction I have with women are the type I pay for. So fucking sue me for wanting one night of normal human interaction for Christ's sake."

Her eyes grow soulful and sad, as if she held a barrier and now she's let it drop.

This girl. *Christ,* what she does to me.

"I—I didn't know," she says, "I shouldn't have jumped to conclusions. I'm sorry."

"There are a lot of things you don't know about me," I say, my anger dwindling when she apologizes. "But one thing you do know, is that I don't take too kindly to women who've agreed to submit to me telling me off for no good reason."

"Um. I do know that," she says, nodding, and hell if she isn't fucking adorable.

"Good," I tell her, taking in a deep, calming breath, then releasing it again. "We'll see how haughty you are when you're belly-down on my bed getting your ass striped with the cane."

"Right," she whispers, looking genuinely afraid. *Good.*

We pull up outside of Verge and cruise to a stop.

I crook a finger at her. "Come here, Cora."

She's responded well to my correction, but this is the first time we're entering the club as dom and submissive, and I want her in her place. I watch her shoulders rise as she takes a deep breath, then crawls her way over to me. Her pretty chin fits perfectly in the palm of my hand as I hold her gaze with mine.

"When we walk in there you stay by my side and keep your head down. This is not a night for socializing. I want you alone in my room immediately. Do you understand?"

"Yes, sir."

"Eyes cast down. I'll take care of anyone who wants to speak to us. If you behave, I'll consider allowing you to visit with your friends in the future. But not tonight. Tonight, it's time we get our roles in order. Understood?"

"Yes, sir."

My stomach warms at that, and my cock lengthens. I love when she submits to me.

"Good," I tell her. "Then maybe after I punish you, we can see about a reward."

"I'd... like that, sir," she says. "I... think."

We exit the car and head to Verge. I watch her closely, and she obeys well, like a good little girl. Eyes cast down, she holds onto my hand and walks by my side. Braxton greets us at the door, looks curiously at Cora, then shoots me a conspiratorial wink.

"Be a good girl tonight, Cora," he yells down the hall after her and to her credit, she doesn't respond. Tobias waves from his office, and when we get to the bar area, Travis gives me a chin lift. He looks from me to Cora, then back to me again, and his jaw tightens. I don't blame him for not trusting me. She's younger and maybe he thinks she's naïve. I meet his eyes and nod at him, conveying what he needs to see.

I've got her. I'll take care of her.

He holds my eyes then finally nods and turns away, a silent move to give us privacy.

"Did Travis give you the evil eye?" she asks quietly. "He's everyone's brother, you know."

"I wouldn't say evil eye, but he definitely was ready to throw down if I hurt you."

Still keeping her head down, I see the faintest glimmer of a smile. "He's a good guy."

My only response is to sweep her hair off her neck and gently wrap my fingers on the bare skin there, collaring her with my hand. I don't need to explain myself to anyone else. The most beautiful submissive in all of NYC is going with me to my private room. Familiar faces see us pass in the dungeon, but I'm beyond caring.

I want her alone.

Stripped.

Naked.

Waiting.

When we get to the navy door, she begins to tremble, but keeps her composure with deep breaths. I tighten my grip on her hand. I won't give her any more comfort quite yet. Tonight is about her obedience to me. My dominance over her. And I won't coddle her.

When we're done, I'll give her what she needs.

I'll hold her as long as she wants me to. Wipe away her tears.

And I know before we even begin, there will be tears.

FIFTEEN

Cora

I DON'T USUALLY COWER when I'm afraid. I don't usually tremble like this or lose my conviction, but when the navy door swings open, I can't bring myself to move. I'm frozen in place like someone's waved a magic wand at me and commanded I stand still. I try to will myself forward, but I can't. Suddenly, the reality of my situation hits me like a gust of wind, and I shiver.

"Let's go, Cora," he says, his voice hard and commanding. "In."

But I can't move.

A sharp crack to my ass makes me gasp like I'm coming up for air, and I quickly find the ability to walk. "Yes, sir. I'm sorry, sir." I don't want to fuck this up. It matters to me that I do this right. He's paying me amply, and I take pride in a job well done.

Tugging me into the room ahead of him, he shuts the door and locks it, then turns to face me.

I have to trust him. I begin to war within myself.

He could hurt you.

But he's a long-term member, and Tobias only allows people he trusts here.

He hasn't hurt you yet and you signed an agreement to this.

Apple. Apple. Apple.

I'm practicing the safeword and I haven't even stripped out of my clothes yet.

Liam's walking around the room and I'm not sure what he's doing, then I realize he's flicked on some background music and lit a flameless candle. A little ambiance? Pressing a button on a little while machine I haven't seen before, he dabbles with the settings until the machine produces a light wisp of air, like smoke, and the room soon is filled with scent of sandalwood and vanilla.

"What are you doing?" I ask curiously.

"Just helping you relax," he says, right before he turns to me. "Sometimes setting the scene can help frame the right sort of mood."

"I see."

He sits on the edge of the bed, his collar unfastened, all sophisticated and sexy-disheveled. When he crooks a finger at me, I swallow hard, take a breath, and head to him. His hands anchor on my hips, and he guides me to stand between his knees. In silence, he begins to strip me. First, a gentle tug at the hem of my top, which he lifts over my head and gently tosses to the edge of the bed. I shiver.

"Are you cold, sweetheart?" God, the gentle tone makes my throat get all tingly. It's disconcerting how he assumes this role as if it's the most natural thing in the world.

"No, sir."

"Good," he whispers. "And soon, I'll warm you up anyway." A soft kiss to my shoulder. My neck. Silky, warm lips on my collarbone then the very top of my breast. I love the feel of his hands spanning my waist, and then lower still, he's slowly divesting me of every strip of clothing until I'm standing between his legs bared.

"Go to the red glass case next to the sideboard."

How did I miss this case before? I must've been in a sex-induced coma, or maybe this is new, because this case is really freaking scary. I don't even know what half these things are, but I know their purpose. Paddles, straps, and canes sit on a velvet cushion, as if they're a display in a gallery, and not spanking implements for impact play at a sex club.

I reach it and look down at them, suddenly feeling both hot and cold at the same time. I wonder what each one feels like and make it my mission to research more heavily. I want to know what I'm facing.

Though his voice is calm, his instruction makes me shiver. "Choose a cane, please."

I swallow hard. "They're... the wicked little thin things, aren't they?"

"They are."

One looks like it's wooden and another plastic or... something. "I... don't know anything about them, sir," I say. "I'm not really sure which to pick."

"A cane is a thin, supple, rod-like implement meant to concentrate impact, therefore increasing the severity of a spanking."

Gah!

"Um. Well, I don't want to be rude, but I knew that much. I mean, I don't know which one means...what."

"You may test them."

"Test them?" I ask, spinning around to look at him. "Like how?"

A corner of his lips quirks up, though his eyes are still stern. "If you think you can test one on me, you can perish *that* thought. To test an implement, it helps to tap it on your palm or thigh."

"Oh. Right," I say flushing. I lift the edge of the case and remove the stout wooden one. It weighs hardly anything at all and feels wicked in my hand, like a magic wand capable of destruction. I gently close the case and tap the cane it on my palm with a little *whoosh*. My skin lights with fire and I gasp. *Shit.* Oh, God. This isn't going to be fun.

Quickly, I test each one, until he sighs with impatience. "Your time is up."

There's no easy choice here. I choose a clear red one with a handle.

"Ah, the acrylic. A fair choice. Now hold the cane in both hands and stand in the corner."

Oh, lovely. He's really into drawing this out.

I walk to the corner where he points, dragging the little weapon in my hand, and when I reach the corner, I stand with my nose against it as he instructed, either end of the cane resting in my palms.

The strings of a violin play in the background, the vanilla scent in the air warm and soothing. I swallow hard and finger the edges of the cane, closing my eyes to try to get into the right mindset, but what really is the right mindset?

I'm so preoccupied I don't hear him approach until I feel him behind me, his hands on my elbows and his mouth to my ear. I jump, but the sound of his voice quickly calms me. "Tonight, you'll be caned for not taking your safety seriously. I've warned you about this, and I want you thinking about how important it is to follow my instructions."

I nod. "Yes, sir."

"Imagine the swing and swish of the cane when I punish you. Each stroke will strip away some of what you've got welled up in here." He presses his palm against my chest, but the touch isn't sexual. Though I'm naked, it's more like an embrace than anything else. My heartbeat thumps against his palm. "Whatever troubled you when you were home, that you let fester and burn until you needed to attack me when we were alone? Bring that out to the surface, so when I punish you, we begin again."

I don't really understand what's going on. I get what he's saying, but those things I have *welled up inside me* are battered down and hidden, like secrets tucked into chests with iron padlocks. I can't just conjure them up like that. It isn't that easy.

"I feel your hesitation, Cora. What is it?"

"I... I don't know how I'm supposed to drag those things up." I feel a little irritated, but I don't really get why, so I just let myself speak without trying to censor my thoughts. "I mean... I agreed to be your submissive. I didn't agree to go to therapy or whatever the fuck."

He's kneading my shoulders with his firm, strong hands, plying the taut muscles, and a little bit of my worry dissipates before I can even begin to hold it back.

"Submitting physically is one thing, Cora," he says. "And mentally is another."

"Why would I submit mentally to you?" I ask. "Hell, I don't even know what that means. And I don't know if I agreed to it."

"Oh, but you did," he says, dragging his hands from my shoulders down my back. "When you signed the contract."

"Where? Was there fine print I missed?" I try to pass it off as a joke, but he isn't amused, and neither am I.

"You agreed to obey me. I've instructed you to

bring your anger that's directed at me to mind. It's a simple request, but not an easy one. Now I'm going to give you some time here to think about what I just said."

And then he's gone, and I feel the loss keenly.

I stand with the cane, the darkened room cast in shadows when I stand in the corner. This isn't anything at all what I expected, but I'm doing myself no favors holding back. Time ticks by so long, that after a while I imagine I can even hear the ticking of a clock, but there is none. I stand with my back rigid, but I'm beginning to grow tired. Though he hasn't instructed me not to move, I have the distinct impression that if I do, he'll punish me.

I'm waiting for his command, but none comes.

Then with no warning at all, something shifts in me. Here, while staring at the blank wall in front of me, there's no visual distraction. With the quiet in the room, the only sound my breathing and his, and the low bubbling sound of the diffuser he put on, my mind begins to quiet. The noise and chatter of my inner thoughts that distract me even in sleep begin to quiet. And when they do, a surprising calm trickles over my skin like warm water. My body heats, and I let out a deep sigh.

"Good girl," he approves from behind me. "Now come here, Cora."

I turn as if waking, suddenly brilliantly aware of every detail. The way he sits on the bed dressed in slacks and a pale blue shirt. The large, masculine hands that rest on his knees. So strong. So powerful. Capable of both destruction and reparation, hands that will master my body. The strong column of his neck, the sharp angle of his jaw, the pronounced slash of his cheekbones. And when I get to his eyes... *God,* those eyes... the depths of blazing blue fixed on mine with nothing but honesty written in those depths.

As I stare at him, his lips thin and his jaw firms.

"I told you to come here, Cora."

I walk quickly toward him, broken from my trance, and as I stand before him, he rolls up his sleeves. It's a beautiful sight, a powerful, silent declaration that he's the one in charge. In control. This is no game.

"Now hand me the cane, please."

Trembling, I obey, sliding the slim implement onto his palm. He stands and points to the bed, wordlessly instructing me to lie over it by tapping the edge with the cane. A full body tremor courses through me as I obey.

"Cora," he says, his palm resting on the small of my back. "Breathe in."

I inhale deeply.

"Now out."

I release the breath.

"Before we begin, tell me what was on your mind while you stood in the corner."

"Well," I tell him honestly. "At first it was everything."

"Everything?"

"Yes. A jumble of thoughts so loud I could

hardly focus on one."

"I see. And then?"

"Then they all began to flit away until my mind grew quiet."

"Good," he says. "That was a test."

"And did I pass?"

"It wasn't pass or fail. I wanted to see if you'd be able to find your peace in the corner, and you were. I'll keep that in mind."

I don't really get it, but I nod into the bed. Now that I'm belly-down and bared to him, and he's standing behind me with that wicked cane in his hand, I sort of want this over with.

"Now tell me the things on your mind."

"I... I don't want to, sir," I say to him, as meekly as I can because I'm not trying to defy him but I'm not super comfortable telling him everything that's on my mind.

"I know you don't. But I asked you to, and I want you to do your best."

This gentle, firm side of Liam unravels me somehow. I don't really know this side of him, but the way he makes me feel inside, I want to.

"Now try, Cora. Why were you so angry at me for being friendly with Bailey and Ben? Start there."

"Because it isn't fair," I tell him. "Our relationship isn't permanent, and I don't want them getting attached to you."

"Good. What else?"

"And... and Ben never had a guy in his life to

look up to or take care of him or teach him guy things, and he's the one I'm super worried about. And Bailey isn't stupid, and she knows something's up with us, but I don't know how to explain anything to her."

"Go on."

"I... I don't know what else to say. At this point I just want you to begin because I know it'll hurt, and I want to get it over with."

"I see." Then he's standing behind me with his hand on my back, and his voice is deeper. Stern. "Why am I going to punish you?"

"I didn't follow your instructions."

"Correct. And what is my rule for you?"

"Obey you," I say in a little voice, squeezing my eyes shut for the smack of the cane. I hear it *whoosh* in the air, and I gasp out loud, flinching when it smacks against my bare ass. Jesus *Christ* that hurts so badly my throat's on fire and I can't breathe.

"Say it again."

"Obey you," I repeat, before a second line of fire slashes across my ass. I whimper this time, unable to hold back my reaction.

"Again."

"Obey you," I whisper, then a third lash of the cane lands.

"Obey you," I say without prompting, before the fourth smack falls. My mind is a muddle of thoughts and protests and there's a lump in my throat like I've just swallowed a bagel sideways.

"I can't!" I protest. "Oh, God, that hurts so

fucking bad!"

"Say it."

"Obey you," I moan, bringing on the fifth swish and thud.

"Obey you!" I scream, just before the last line of fire ignites me. I'm panting, balled up with my fists under my chest, when he sits on the edge of the bed, picks me up, and plants me straight over his lap.

I cringe and squirm when his palm encircles my scorched, aching ass. He murmurs quietly.

"Let it go, Cora. I can feel you taut like a string ready to snap. Let it go, now." And the soft cadence of his voice breaks my resolve more effectively than the most vicious cut of the cane. "You took your punishment like a good girl. Such a very good girl."

He's massaging me, soothing my punished skin, and coaxing the lump in my chest to dissolve. "There is so much that's new to you, but I'm proud of you," he continues, his voice taking on a rougher, more rugged tone. "You're so strong and brave, and knowing you've granted me permission to dom you makes me proud as fuck. You know that?" Over and over, warm strokes of his palm, and as the pain begins to fade, I'm suddenly crying. My eyes are wet and I'm silently weeping, swiping at my eyes so he doesn't see.

"I punished you because I want you to remember this. That you belong to me, and obeying every instruction is crucial. That I won't let harm come to you, and when you—"

He halts mid-sentence, but I'm dimly aware of it, for I'm crying freely now and can't seem to stop. Then he's tucking me into his warm, broad chest, and I'm soaking his shirt clean through. I'm trying to stop the tears, but I can't. It isn't just the punishment he gave me tonight, but something he dredged up from so much deeper below that surface. Rocking me, he holds me tighter, and his final instruction gives me the permission I need.

"Let it all out." It's so tender, I can't hold back. "Like that, little one. You're safe."

I'm completely exposed, as naked and vulnerable as a newborn baby, and I don't even try to stop my tears. I couldn't even if I wanted to, they're coming from a well deep inside me, fathoms below the surface where my darkest torment dwells.

"Shh," is all he says, rocking me against his chest. My nose is dripping and I'm slobbering all over him like a puppy, but he doesn't care and neither do I. For the first time in my adult life, hell, maybe my *whole* life, I'm somehow safe, ironically centered and secure in the arms of the man who just punished me.

"I—I don't know—I didn't mean..." I stammer, my voice thick with emotion.

"You don't need to," he says in my ear, kissing my wet cheeks and damp forehead, and pulling me so close to him it hurts. "You were holding a lot back, and it's come loose, but it's okay now. Don't try to stop now. You're safe here. I've got you."

Somehow, I know it to be true. Our relationship

defies everything my logical brain tells me, and yet, here I am, held close and cherished. Any man who can comfort a sobbing mess like me, who can take my broken pieces laid bare by the strokes of punishment he gave me, has earned something I've given not one solitary soul on this earth. So, I let it go. I cry, and I cry, and I cry, until there are no more tears to be shed. I feel wrung dry like a limp dishcloth, hiccupping against his sopping wet chest, and still he holds me.

"Good girl," he whispers. "Christ, you're brave. You know that?"

How can anyone call a woman who just wept like a child after a spanking *brave?*

"Brave?" I whisper, with a self-deprecating snort. "I just... how can you call me brave?"

"It takes so much courage to do what you just did," he says. "I feel like Neil Fucking Armstrong stepping on the moon."

"What?" I say, suddenly giddy and lighter than I've been in years. I'm laughing while hiccupping from the slobbering sob session I just had. "What do you mean?"

But he doesn't answer. "Never mind that now," he says. "Jesus, woman, what you do to me." He hands me tissues and I unceremoniously blow my nose.

Standing with me still tucked against his chest, he moves slowly and I'm quiet. I don't know what to say or what we do now. I'm exhausted yet buoyant. I want to thank him, and I don't even know why, and the thought of him releasing me right now scares me.

"Don't let me go just yet," I whisper, then remember my manners. "Please, sir?"

"Let you go?" he says. "Hell no. I just found you."

He's laying me on my back on the bed but somehow, he doesn't let go of me. I'm still wrapped in his arms, and he's kneeling above me, one knee on either side, his arms under my back, and he's kissing me. God, he's kissing every inch of me but my mouth. My rumpled hair and wet cheeks and shoulders, and when he comes to my neck, I tip my head to the side and moan. I don't even try to stop myself or hold back but let him ravish me with lips and teeth and tongue. Like a match to tinder, my body ignites. Just a moment ago, the last thing on my mind was sex, but he's so strong, so powerful, so *tender,* I can't help my instinctual arousal. My breasts swell and tingle, my nipples furling when he brushes a knuckle across the tender skin.

"So fucking beautiful," he says. I love how his dignified persona fades at moments like this, as if somehow, unwittingly, I've undone his hard-won decorum. With slow, languid movements, he captures my wrists in his powerful hands and pins them above my head with one hand, the other hand tipping my chin up so he can kiss me. My hips rise to meet him, and I sigh. I don't care about holding back anymore. Hell, I'm not sure I could if I wanted to.

He nips my lip and sucks it into his mouth, still pinning my wrists so tightly I'm powerless to stop anything he does. His mouth moves from my lips back to my cheek, then down to my jaw and back to my neck. I yelp when he sinks his teeth into the tender skin, hard enough to hurt, but the pain sends a bolt of desire between my thighs. A slow graze of his lips to the other side of my neck, and he bites again. This time my clit throbs, and I jerk my hips against him. I can feel the length of him pressed against my pussy. God, I want him to fuck me. Something tells me Liam Alexander fucks the way he wants, and that's exactly what I need right now.

He moves his hand to his pocket, then the next thing I know he's wrapping something soft and silky around my wrists, before he secures the loop on a hook on the bed. My hands are suspended above my head. I shiver when I realize this leaves me completely at his mercy.

"I was going to blindfold you," he says. "To help you let go. But I don't think that's necessary tonight." I shake my head, swallowing hard with what I know is coming. My body's on fire, primed with want, and in that moment, I know the only one who can satisfy that need is him.

"How are you feeling?" he asks.

"Horny as fuck," I rasp.

He shoots me a wolfish grin and nods. "Perfect."

I watch him strip, my mouth dry, unabashedly taking in every glorious detail of his exquisite body.

This is no show, though, as he looks away and carelessly tosses his clothes to the floor. As if he doesn't know how hot he is, all strength and muscles, this big strapping man who just punished me then held me with the gentlest touch has me so ready to take him. I'm no virgin, but I've never slept with a real man.

"It's funny to me that you have tattoos," I tell him, letting my eyes lazily roam the black markings that snake up his arms.

Shrugging, he mutters. "A drunken effort to piss off my mother."

"Did it work?"

"Oh yeah," he says. "She screeched like a banshee and told me she was writing me out of the will."

"Good," I tell him. "For what it's worth, I approve."

He's stripped to his boxers now, the length of his erection making me swallow hard with nerves. Like everything about Liam, he's huge.

"For what it's worth?" he repeats with a wry smile. "I'm glad you do."

I grin at him, and he smiles back, and in that moment, we're more than two people with a contract. And then my mind goes hazy and my body takes over, because he's on me, and he smells so fucking good, and hell, this man knows how to touch me.

"There are so many things I want to do to you."

"Oh yeah, handsome?" I whisper. I want to

know what I'm in for, and I want him to do those things to me.

"Hot wax," he says. "Christ, how gorgeous you'll look covered with wax."

"Sounds... painful," I say with a smile. "But I'm game."

"Doesn't have to be painful," he says, his breath hot on my cheek. I gasp when he draws his tongue along my cheekbone and moans. "I want to lick every inch of you. The taste of your pussy haunts my fucking dreams."

"Jesus," I whisper, so turned on I think if he breathes on my pussy I'll climax. "What else do you want to do?"

"Clamps," he says.

"Fair."

"Shibari."

"Oooh. That's the rope thing?"

He chuckles, dragging his tongue to the valley of my breasts, and I catch my breath. "Yeah, baby. That's the rope thing."

"What exactly do you *do* after I'm tied up, though?"

The ravenous grin he gives me makes my heart take a tumble. "Anything I fucking want."

He dips his mouth to my breast and pulls my nipple between his teeth so hard it hurts. I arch when he suckles and laves my breast.

"Fuck," I moan. "Jesus." It's torturous and beautiful. I want him to stop and I need him not to.

The contradictions he draws out in me leave me panting with need.

Pinching and kneading my left breast while he suckles and nips my right, he grinds his erection against me. I rise to meet him, and want to touch him, but a tug of my wrists reminds me I'm still tied. Then he's moving lower, to my belly, and I don't want his mouth there because I don't like my belly. But I can't tell him that, because I'm not allowed and I have to stay right here, in this moment, liking what I can and letting go of what I can't control.

And somewhere, deep inside me, where my fears lay... I want that.

"I can feel you tensing, Cora," he warns. Can he?

"You're fucking beautiful. Say it."

"Liam..."

"Say. It."

But I can't, the words are caught in my throat and I don't know how to let them free.

"Do you want another round with the cane?"

Is he joking? Would he *really?*

"No, but I—you wouldn't!"

"Sure as hell would. I'm totally fucking serious." And he is. I can tell by the way his voice grows hard and his eyes meet mine.

"I... but you..."

"You do what I say," he says, with a warning slap to my thigh. "You get one more chance before I get the cane."

"Oh my God," I tell him. "You're ruthless."

"Sweetheart, I've only just begun."

"Okay, okay, I—" I close my eyes and say it in one breath. "I'm beautiful."

My reward is a swipe of his tongue though my swollen folds.

"Ohmigod."

"Say it again."

I shake my head and he bites my inner thigh, so I scream out without thinking, "I'm beautiful!"

He plunges fingers in my core and pumps once, twice, three times. My back arches and I ache with need for him.

"Again."

"I'm beautiful," I choke out, hardly able to breathe, because he's suckling my clit while pumping his fingers in me, and I might die if I don't come like *right now.*

He takes his mouth off me just long enough to repeat. "Again, Cora."

"I'm beautiful," I whisper as he glides his body up mine and holds me to his chest.

"I'm beautiful," I whisper without the prompting this time, because I know that every time I say this now he rewards me, and fuck, I want that reward. His cock is hot at my entrance, gliding through my folds, then he's stroking the head along my clit.

"I'm beautiful," I groan, then he glides into me and it's so fucking perfect I moan. I'm full and I can't think straight, I'm tight around him and consumed all at once, and every thrust builds friction that might split me in two but I don't care, because my chest is full to bursting and my body's ignited with flames.

"You're beautiful," he whispers in my ear.

And as I look down at my body molded to his, my curvy thighs wrapped around his hips, my vision blurs and my mind come to a stuttering halt, because in that moment, at the very precipice of ecstasy when my heart thumps erratically and I'm panting against him, my wrists held above me and my body connected to his...

"I'm beautiful," I whisper, and for the first time, I believe it. His rhythm quickens and my thighs quiver before my body takes over. I moan in his ear and he's grunting and panting in mine, chasing carnal need and pleasure as I ride out the waves of bliss. I pull my wrists just to feel the resistance, I love that I can't stop this even if I wanted to.

Panting. Heavy breaths. Damp skin and racing hearts. He drops his forehead to my chest and breathes out, then in, holding me tight against him. After seconds or minutes or hours, he finally lifts his head and grins at me.

"That was fucking awesome, beautiful."

I grin up at him, feeling free and lighter than I have in years, but I don't want to think about that now. He's torn me apart then stitched me back together again, but I still feel frail, like I might come apart at the seams again. "It was. Now, my wrists, please, sir."

SIXTEEN

Liam

IT'S six o'clock on Friday night, the sixth week of our contract, and I'm heading to the bookstore. I've had Cora at Verge every night this week, and my appetite's nowhere near satisfied. The more I taste of her the more I want, until she's infiltrated my every-waking thought. I lose track of my focus during meetings, imagining what I'll do to her next when I have her at Verge. I wake up in the morning and send her a text or call, depending on whether or not she's home or heading into class. At night, the separation is nearly painful, but she has to get back to Ben and Bailey, and I have to respect that.

And now I'm at the bookstore for the first time in weeks.

The last time I came here, she mouthed off to

me and I fantasized about striping her ass for her defiance and teaching her to mind her mouth, but now in retrospect I recognize I was a prick. It's surprising how much can change in such a short span of time. I'm sure many would still call me a prick, to be honest. I don't care about being nice in business, I'm still ruthless when it comes to closing deals. But Cora... hell, she's softened a part of me I didn't even know was there.

It's dangerous as hell, and I know it. But I can't seem to stop myself. When I set my eyes on what I want, I get it, and I don't let anything get in my way.

And I've set my eyes on Cora.

I get out of the car and head into the coffee shop, but I don't see her at first.

"Hey, Liam." Marla's stacking books on a display in the center of the room.

I nod to her. "Hey, is Cora here?"

"Yep. She just stepped out back for a minute to grab some sale carts. You can go back if you'd like."

"Thank you," I tell her. God, I can't wait to see her again, and it's only been a few hours. "I've got a favor to ask you, though. Any chance Cora can take off early?"

"Of course," she says with a smile. "Chandra will be here any minute, and I'm closing tonight. You've got plans?"

I show her what I've got stowed in my pocket, and she claps her hands.

"Go ask her," she says, urging me on.

"Hey," I say, pushing open the storeroom door. Cora's balancing precariously on a step ladder that wobbles beneath her, trying to reach for something on a top shelf. Is she crazy? She's barely got a grip and if she falls—

"Hey," she says, standing on one foot and reaching so high, I'm afraid she's gonna topple over. I sprint to the ladder.

"What the hell are you doing?" I ask her. "Get your ass down here."

Trained to obey me, she shoots me a curious look. "Well nice to see you, too," she says with a frown. "Why are you getting your knickers all up in a wad?"

Oh no she did not.

"My *knickers?* Swear to God, Cora, if you don't get your ass own here—"

"Liam, please," she says. "I've almost got it." She shakes her head and reaches higher, then loses her balance, giving a little shriek. She wobbles on the ladder and scrambles for purchase, and finally gets her footing, panting.

"Now," I tell her.

"Okay, okay," she says, shooting me a guilty glance that says she knows she's in trouble, and she's barely touched bottom before I've got her up in my arms, over my shoulder, and I'm smacking the underside of her ass with my palm.

"If you ever do that again," I tell her, with another resounding *smack,* followed by another and another.

"You will do your classwork standing, because you won't sit down for a damn month!" I give her another good, hard spank that makes her arch her back. The satisfying sting in my palm makes my anger abate a little. I slide her down off my shoulder to standing in front of me. Her cheeks match her hair, flaming red, and she rubs her ass adorably.

It's nothing like the spankings she's taken at Verge, but I think I've gotten my point across.

"*Liam*," she hisses. "I'm at *work*."

"And your boss is a submissive who ought to have her own ass whipped for having such a hazard in her stockroom," I tell her, unrepentant.

"Well," she says thoughtfully. "Her last dom actually did try to get rid of the thing, but she's stubborn and he moved away, so..."

I give her a stern glare, lifting my phone and swiping it on.

"Hello?" Mandy answer on the first ring.

"Mandy, order the most stable stock room ladder you can," I tell her, giving her the location while I hold Cora's gaze. I place the order and she shakes her head, but she's subdued after her little spanking, so she doesn't say anything. Satisfied, I slide my phone into my pocket.

"Well," she says. "Might want to run that by Marla?"

"Oh, I'll run that by Marla alright," I tell her. I have every intention of *running it by Marla*. Marla isn't my sub, but she works with *my* woman—

alright, my woman *for now*—and I have a few things to say about safety.

And then Cora grins and I want to pull her to my chest and kiss that mouth of hers until she forgets what she's doing in here in the first place.

"Why are you here?" she says. "I didn't think I'd see you until my shift was over."

"Well, I had a change in plans," I tell her. I pull the pair of rectangular tickets out of my pocket. "What do you think? Want to go on a real date?"

I don't know what reaction I expected, but it isn't what she does. I watch as her eyes fill with tears and she takes the tickets in her hand. "You got tickets to *Chicago?* How'd you even know? These have been sold out for months..."

I shrug. I happened to notice a post on her Instagram page about how it's on her bucket list to go, and "sold out" is a relative term when you've got enough money to get what you want. The past few weeks have been... Jesus, I don't even know.

Magical. Enchanted.

"Don't cry, baby," I tell her, wiping her tears with the pad of my thumb. "Your grades this semester were incredible, and I'm proud of you. You deserve a little celebration."

"You're proud of me?" she repeats, her chin wobbling. "Oh, Liam." And then she dives into my chest and hugs me so tightly I lose my breath.

"The show's at eight, so we've got to get going. You need to get ready, and we'll make sure Bailey and Ben are all set for tonight. Okay?"

"Okay, yeah."

"Marla already agreed."

"Wow," she says. "You really have thought of everything, haven't you?"

I respond by pulling her to me and kissing her, then letting her go with pat to the ass. "Get a move on, woman. Broadway doesn't wait."

After she grabs her bag and we say good-bye to Marla, we head to her place. She chatters the whole time about the cast and story, but I don't really give a shit about the cast and story. I care that her eyes light up like stars in a jewel-studded sky. I care that when she's happy she gets animated like this, talking too quickly and speaking with her hands. I let her chatter on until I finally pull her onto my lap and silence her with another kiss.

"Oh my," she says when I let her go. "Someone's getting lucky tonight."

I tug a lock of her hair and smile. "I get lucky whenever the hell I want."

"This is true," she says with a smirk. "But not for long. Soon, that contract's up, then what're you gonna do, big guy?" Though she's teasing, there's question in her eyes. But I don't have an answer to that question.

What am I gonna do indeed?

"Steal you away," I tell her. "Lock you up in cuffs in my office so you can't leave me." And even though I'm teasing her, my stomach tightens because I don't like the idea of her being apart from me.

I've never cared about anyone *leaving* me before. I was always the one who walked away.

But with Cora? Hell, this is different.

"I'm not going anywhere, Liam," she says quietly, but we don't get to talk anymore about it, because we're pulling up to her apartment building, and she's got to get ready.

"Want me to come up?" I ask her. I don't like to go up unless she grants me permission. And sometimes she still prefers to have some privacy with Bailey and Ben. I get that.

"Yeah," she says, "if you don't mind." Shooting me a sheepish grin, she tucks her head. "Honestly, Liam, Ben's been asking for you."

"Why didn't you tell me?" I say, getting out of the car with her and taking her by the hand. This time, there's no screeching landlord to interrupt us, because I sent that bitch a check to cover six month's rent with a nice little note telling her scarcity around Cora would be a really fantastic decision.

"Well, you're busy," she says.

"Is that really it?"

She's much better about being honest with me these days, and I like to think I'm better about reading her. I know there's more to it than my busyness.

"He talks about you a lot... I'm worried he's getting attached," she says quietly, as we enter her apartment building. I step around a couple making out in the hallway with disgust and lift her right up and over a guy vaping on his back under the stairwell with his legs jetting out.

Jesus, she was right about not bringing me in here. I don't give a shit about her furniture or the too-thin walls, but I do care about her safety.

She isn't yours.

The fuck she isn't.

I can't bother about that now, though. I can't let it eat at me, because Cora isn't mine for the keeping.

"We only have two weeks left to our contract, Liam," she says, and right before we get to her door, she turns and faces me. Dropping her voice, that wobbles a little when she speaks, she places her palm on my chest. I wonder if she can feel the hammering of my heart. I don't want to talk to her about this. I don't want to face it.

"I know," I tell her.

"And I—" her voice trails off. She swallows, inhales, then raises her eyes to mine. "I don't want him getting too attached. You know that."

"Yeah," I tell her.

She's worried about a ten-year-old boy getting attached? Hell, I don't know how *I'm* going to handle it when our contract is up and I'm a full-grown man.

A full-grown man who's in danger of breaking his own fucking contract.

Cora freezes when she looks at the bottom of the door. Smoke creeps out in tendrils.

Shit.

Shoving her key in, she yanks the door open, and billows of smoke fill the hallway. She tries to get in ahead of me, but I shove her behind me and barge in.

"Hey! What's going on in here?"

"Oh, God, Liam," Bailey moans. She's standing in front of the stove and there are flames leaping out of it.

"Get out of the way," I order. "Cora, get them in the hall."

Smoke chokes me and I hear them scrambling behind me. Blinded, I squint my eyes and look for something to put the flames out but there's nothing. The stove stands between me and the sink, and I can't get to the water.

"Liam, get out of there!" Cora yells. "It's climbing up the cupboards and they could fall on you!" I look quickly and realize this isn't some small kitchen fire, but it's already progressed to serious.

I turn to look at Cora when something falls and hits me. I get to the floor and cover my head when I look into the hall and see the sign *fire extinguisher*.

"Get the fire extinguisher!" I yell to her.

"There's nothing there!" she shouts. "It's empty! Ben!"

"Where is he?" Jesus, I thought he was with Bailey but in the confusion, he's run back in for something. I see his blue sneakers below the smoke and push myself to standing, choking on the fumes.

"Get the hell out of here," I growl at him and

reach for him, but he darts away, screaming something about his bag. Jesus.

I run after him and grab him by the back of the shirt, yank him to me, and shove him toward the door. We get to the hallway just in time, as the kitchen literally crashes and falls to pieces behind us. Huge flames engulf the entire little area.

"Get out of here!" I tell Cora. "You make sure Bailey's safe, I've got Ben!"

"Fire!" Cora yells, taking Bailey with her. Doors are opening and people start shouting. There should be building alarms going off, and fire engines one their way but why am I surprised this place isn't up to code? I drag Ben beside me. He's crying and soot runs down his cheeks, and I feel bad for getting mad at him. Kids don't think when they're in danger. Hell, that's why they need parents to take care of them.

I've got three people coming to my place tonight.

I call 911 on my phone when we get outside, and we spend hours answering questions. The police officer interrogating Bailey tries to give her shit, but when he sees me, he gets his act together. Bailey insists she was doing her homework in her room with her earbuds in, and she had a tray of frozen macaroni and cheese in the oven. The next thing she knew, smoke was creeping under her door. She ran out to see what was going on, and the kitchen was in flames.

"Did you have anything on the stove?"

"No, officer," she says. "Nothing at all."

"You're her father?" The officer asks, giving me a once-over.

Father? Jesus *God*. The idea... Well, hell, I guess I can't blame him for thinking that though. She looks like a kid and I'm much older than she is.

"No," I tell him. "Sister's boyfriend." I tell him my side of the story.

"There was nothing on the stove, I swear," she says. "I'm super careful about those things."

Finally, he leaves them alone. I make sure the fire department knows there were no fire extinguishers or alarms that went off, and they ask me for my name for questioning.

I give him my business card, and he whistles. "Liam Alexander," he says. "Of Alexander Enterprises?"

"Yeah."

"What are you doing in a place like this?" he asks.

Asshole.

Cora flinches and I clench my jaw.

"Call me with any questions about the fire," I tell him, then turn to Cora, Bailey, and Ben. We could go to a hotel or some other place for the night, but after this ordeal, I want Cora with me, and I want her brother and sister to have more security than a transient hotel room. "You three are coming home with me."

SEVENTEEN

Cora

SO, suffice it to say, this wasn't how I thought the night would go.

I went from mentally cataloging my closet of clothes Liam's bought for me to choose the best outfit to wear to the play, from watching Ben and Bailey slide into his car with wide-eyes, their cheeks still smudged with soot, their clothes a wreck.

And now we're heading to Liam's place.

Just. *Great.*

"We need to get them checked out, Liam," I say gently.

I don't know what's going to happen in a couple of weeks, but I will never forget seeing that man pull my brother out of that apartment. *Ever.* God, what he's doing to me is dangerous as all hell, but I can't stop it. I mean, I'm only human.

"Don't worry about it," he says. "I'll call my doctor and have him pay a visit." Well, yeah. Of course, he has a doctor that does house calls. I don't know why this surprises me.

Turning to Ben, he lowers his voice. "You alright?"

He leans over and ruffles Ben's hair, and it makes my heart squeeze a little.

"Yeah," Ben says quietly, but his face is all rumpled like he's about to cry. "But what about my bag? And my Legos? And *your* stuff?" he says, turning to me. "All those pretty clothes you got? You didn't have a lot of those and now they're gone."

"Hey, we don't know that," I say to him. "Maybe they put out the fire before all our stuff was destroyed," but Liam gently shakes his head at me as if to warn me not to make promises I can't keep.

"Stuff's replaceable," Liam says. "People are not."

And hell, for some reason, just hearing him say those words? Right then, right there, I've broken rule number six and I know it.

I love this man. Jesus, I love him. And there isn't a damn thing I can do about it.

I told myself he was a jerk, and I really thought he was. I told myself this was just a business arrangement. I'm not sure when it ceased being one, but there's more than a superficial exchange of power here.

"I agree with Liam," I say to them, though my voice is wavering. They're my brother and sister, and I'm not their mom, but it feels right having Liam by my side through this. "Liam's right. Let's get settled at Liam's—" and then I remember. "Oh, Liam." My heart sinks. "The play." We'll miss it now, and the knowledge makes me want to cry, but I have to stay strong. Things happen.

He reaches for my hand and gives it a little squeeze. "It's okay," he says. "I promise. I'll make it better."

Can he, though? Can he really make it all better?

I like that he wants to, though.

I watch Bailey's eyes go wide as she takes in the luxurious layout of his car. Not quite a limo, it's still huge inside. The backseat has two rows of seats that face each other like a limo would. Hell. Maybe this *is* a limo, just a slimmer model for navigating the streets of NYC.

"This is some fancy car," Bailey say. "I kinda can't wait to see what your place looks like."

Me neither. It's a little weird to me that I've already made up my mind I love the guy, and I've never stepped foot in his apartment. This wasn't how things were supposed to go at all. He was never supposed to go into *my* apartment, and now here we are with Bailey and Ben and heading toward his. But life has a funny way of tricking us, sometimes. Of letting us think we have control, when we really are only along for the ride.

"Yeah, for real," Ben says. "Do you have like servants and stuff?"

Liam smiles and strokes his chin as if he's trying to remember. "Yeah," he says. "I suppose I do."

"What do they do?" Ben asks, his large eyes wide. He doesn't seem so afraid anymore.

"Whatever I tell them."

Bailey gives me a smirk and I narrow my eyes at her to tell her not to even think about saying anything.

"I've got someone who cooks for me," he says to Ben. "Someone who cleans. Someone who drives. It's just the way it goes."

"Woooowww," Ben says. "Do you rent out movie theaters when you go? Do you have like a diamond on the home button for your iPhone? Have you ever owned a *solid* brick of *gold?*"

I burst out laughing at the image of any of these things. "Is that what you think rich people do?" I ask, and Liam's laughing, too.

"Not much of a fan of movie theaters," he tells Ben. "I like to watch movies at home. Gold bricks? No, but I've seen and held them. As for diamonds, I can think of much better uses for them than to bling up an iPhone." His eyes meet mine and hold them for a second. I breathe in and out not saying anything, because I'm not sure if he meant to imply what he did or maybe he didn't imply anything at all. Maybe I'm just lovesick and silly and I need to get myself together.

It's a good drive to his place in uptown Manhattan, and by the time we get there, we're all starving, and quiet, not having really processed the loss we've sustained, but curious what will happen next. This is a part of NYC I don't see much of. There are no broken sidewalks or graffiti on the walls. There are no people making out on the stairs and landlords reaming people out on the street.

A few couples walk by, one dressed in casual but simple clothing, another holding hands and dressed as if they're going to the Oscars. I feel suddenly silly in my worn jeans and sweater I had on from the bookstore.

"Do you have clothes upstairs?" Bailey asks me. "Stuff in his place?"

"No," I tell her honestly. "I've never been here." But I don't elaborate. She knows we meet at a club sometimes, but she doesn't need to know what kind of a club it is, so I try to tell her as much as I can without revealing too much. "He has a room at the club, and I keep things there, though."

"I see." She lifts her brows and looks from me to him and back again. She knows there are things I don't want to tell her, and I hope she can respect that. It's for her benefit as much as it's for mine.

Manuel comes around to open the door, and I'm suddenly aware of what a big deal this is for Bailey and Ben. They've never seen luxury. I've been spoiled by Liam these past few weeks, and even though I've taken care of them as best I can with what he's paid me, it's nothing like really seeing firsthand how other people live.

"Wow," Ben breathes, his eyes widening at the sight of a gorgeous red Ferrari parked at the curb.

"Wow is right," Bailey says, craning her neck to look to the top of his building, then moving her head from side to side to take in as much as she can. "Liam, take us in!"

"Come on. This way," Liam says, and I can't read his expression. Is he proud or embarrassed? Both? Or something else altogether? I don't know what he's thinking. I feel like we're really invading his privacy, and I have no idea how long we'll stay here. I'm not even sure he wants us to. We could've easily gone to a hotel, but for some reason he chose to bring us here. But he's ushering us into the building, where a man in a suit bows his head to greet him so it's not a great time to ask him.

"Mr. Alexander," he says. "Guests tonight?"

"Yes, thank you." We go inside the building and Ben and Bailey look at every detail with wide-open mouths. Hell, I can hardly keep my own jaw from dropping.

The foyer on the main floor has a small but beautiful waterfall, lit from behind with pale pink and white lights. Gentle strings of violin play in the background, and there's a uniformed gentleman sitting at the main desk who waves a hand in greeting to Liam.

"Joseph," Liam says, bringing us up to the desk,

but Ben's over by the waterfall reaching a tentative finger out to touch it. He's completely oblivious to us over by the desk.

"Oh, for crying out loud," I mumble. It's bad enough we've come in here disheveled and a mess. I don't need to draw any more attention to how poorly we fit in here. "Ben! Ben *get over here.*" But he ignores me.

Liam turns and calls out in his much deeper voice, "Ben, over here." Ben looks at us, and trots over to join us. Bailey and I share a rolling-eye look. Ben adores Liam, and when he meets us, he stands right next to him.

"Joseph, we need to give these three access until we have a place for them to stay. They'll be with me."

Ok, wait. We didn't talk about this.

"Liam, we didn't discuss this," I tell him. "I mean I don't know that we need keys or access cards or whatever. I don't want you to have to—"

He shakes his head at me. "I know, and we will talk about it, but for now, you all need to be able to get in, even if you're just here for the night, okay?"

"Okay," I say reluctantly. "Yeah, I guess that's fine."

"I don't want to be here just for the night," Ben protests, looking back at the waterfall and the sprawling foyer. "If it looks this nice down here, what does it look like in his place?"

Liam chuckles, but Bailey goes beet red. "*Ben.*"

I just sigh. I want us settled and these two

taken care of. And hell, I want to be taken care of myself. I need to be alone with Liam and I'm still mentally adjusting to the change in plans.

We go upstairs on an elevator that looks like it could launch a spaceship. Ben takes in every detail in wide-eyed silence as Liam introduces us to the elevator operator.

"Why do you have someone push buttons for you?" he asks Liam. "I mean, that's kind of an easy thing to do."

I open my mouth to stop him, but Liam just rolls with it. "It's fine, Cora. He'll have a lot of questions and there's nothing wrong with that." Liam says something to him about tradition and service, but I'm not paying attention. There are too many questions in my mind. Too much uncertainty. And my biggest fears of Ben getting attached to Liam are now pronounced, because Liam's wowing Ben without even trying.

The elevator arrives on his floor, and the operator tips his hat to us. A slim hallway stands between his entrance and the elevator, and it feels like this is sort of monumental. Liam taking me home is a far cry from him taking me to Verge. At Verge, I could at least tell myself that I am his paid submissive for the night or the week or whatever. Here, however... Here it is different.

This is welcoming me into a part of his life he's never let me see before. This is an intimacy we haven't yet shared, and I wonder where this will leave us as we move to the latter part of our contract.

Fucking contract.

I don't pay attention to the opulent details of the hallway as he brings us to the entryway and opens the door.

"*Holy crap,*" Ben breathes, when we all step foot inside his penthouse. I say nothing, as I take in every detail in stunned silence and Ben's sort of already voiced my own reaction.

I knew Liam was rich. But this... this is unlike anything I ever imagined.

Past the entryway is a massive living room with floor to ceiling windows, looking out on the brightly lit Manhattan skyline. Shades of lights in blues and blacks and white glitter like gems, the magnificent buildings glow, a real-life work of art. Ivory sofas face each other, modern looking crescent-shaped pieces that somehow manage to look both swanky and comfortable aside a gleaming black baby grand piano. A large fireplace dwarfs one wall to the right, and beyond the fireplace is a spiral staircase that must lead to the upstairs bedrooms. Under the staircase lies a doorway to another bedroom. Liam's? To the left is the entryway to the kitchen, which I can't really see because it's cast in darkness.

I kick my shoes off and silently beckon Bailey and Ben to do the same. They follow suit, still taking in every detail they can. Liam shrugs out of his suit coat and hangs it up in a closet by the door, then takes my hand and pulls me in.

"I'll give you the tour," he says, with a smirk. Waving his hand around, he says, "This is it." I giggle.

"Charming."

"You guys make yourselves at home. I'll get us something to eat and call the doctor to check you out. Then we'll sort sleeping arrangements." Liam's on his phone already, taking charge, and hell I love that. Ben and Bailey are already standing by the large windows, so they miss the way he pinches my ass. I feel heat creeping along my neck at the knowledge that I'll probably share his bed tonight.

It all passes in a blur. I can't wrap my brain around Liam in the kitchen, heating up a tray of lasagna and serving it with a salad. It looks almost domestic, and it clashes with my mental image of him, but it feels nice. Natural. Homey. And I haven't had those feelings in quite some time. It feels domestic and comfortable, and we laugh when Ben asks if the glasses we're drinking out of are made of diamond. Still, I make sure I'm the one loading the dishwasher, and not Ben.

Ben takes one small bedroom at the top of the stairs and Bailey the other, Liam's doctor visits about an hour after we've eaten, and on Liam's instruction, Manuel brings us all pajamas and toothbrushes and chargers for our phones. When we're settled, he calls NYPD for an update that he promises he'll give me later, then tells us all tomorrow, after a good night's sleep and breakfast, we'll get more of what we need. He's thought of everything, it seems, and he seems happy in this role, taking care of us like this. I suppose it makes sense, as he's a dominant, and I know I've talked to Beatrice and Diana about how Zack and Tobias are similar. They enjoy taking charge. They're happiest when the people they care about are well then care of.

People they care about.

Does that mean Liam cares about us?

And finally, after a surreal whirlwind of getting things situated until Ben and Bailey go to bed... I collapse on the pretty crescent sofa. Liam's in the kitchen, pouring us each a glass of wine, when he comes to join me.

"Been a long day for you, sweetheart."

I rest my head on his shoulder and take a long pull from my glass. "It has. God, this wine tastes good."

"I'm glad you like it."

"What kind is it?"

"Ah, who the hell knows. If I like it, I tell Lila the chef, and she keeps me well stocked."

It makes sense. He doesn't have time for such plebeian things like grocery shopping.

He's lit a fire though it isn't that cold outside, but it lends an ambiance to the room that I like. I watch the flames flicker on the wall and sip my wine. It isn't until then, when I'm relaxed and alone with Liam, that I really, truly feel my exhaustion. It suffuses my limbs and my eyes are heavy. Though the past few weeks have been really amazing, I've been going full throttle. And it wasn't until our safety was truly in jeopardy that I felt the weight of what I've been carrying.

Liam's changed into a t-shirt and a pair of jeans, his socked feet stretched out by the fire, crossed at his ankles.

"Happy Friday," he says. "Not what we planned, but hell if I don't like having you here with me. This place always feels too big. But tonight, it doesn't."

I don't reply at first, because I'm not really sure what I want to say to him. Instead, I excuse myself to go check on the kids. I hand him my glass and walk up the spiral staircase.

Ben's already fast asleep, in a pair of navy blue pjs, tucked into a queen-sized bed. God, how I wish this was his reality. How I wish we didn't have to return to that dilapidated, stinking building with that witch of a landlord. I tuck the blanket around him, and he wakes up, blinking sleepy eyes up at me. "This is like a mansion," he says with a big yawn. "It's nice." Then he's fast asleep again. A lump rises in my throat, but I swallow it down.

Am I making a mistake? In my attempts to take care of them, bringing them to his place, will I hurt them? I don't like the idea of them getting any more attached to him than they already are.

Sighing, I make my way to the next room. Ben's room is a guest room, but Bailey's is simpler. It's a small office of sorts, with a comfortable pull-out sofa for her to sleep on. She's sitting up, reading something on her phone when I walk in.

"Hey," she says, smiling at me. "Wow, this place is nice, huh?"

"Yeah," I say. "It's pretty good."

"I'm afraid of breaking something, though."

"Me, too," I say with a laugh. I look out the door. From here, I can see the very top of the large windows in the living room. "But at least we're safe now."

"Yeah," she says. "Did Liam get in touch with the police?"

"Yeah. He'll fill us in later. There were no fire alarms or extinguishers like there were supposed to be in the hallway, and I bet we haven't heard the end of this. They're likely going to condemn the building. But we'll see."

"Oh, wow," she says. "Where do people... go... and stuff? Will we be able to get our things?"

"I don't know where people will go, but the city has many shelters, and most people will likely stay with friends or relatives for now. As for our things, yes, we'll be able to fetch them sometime this weekend, I'm guessing."

"I didn't start that fire, Cora," she says. It isn't until she states it that I even realize she feared that.

"You didn't. They're still investigating, but it was very clearly faulty lines in the stove that caused that fire." The reality of what could've happened hits me in the chest, and my eyes fill with tears.

"I'm just so glad you guys are okay," I tell her, brushing her hair off her forehead gently.

"Me, too," she whispers. "But are you?"

Am I? God, I have no idea.

"I'm fine, honey," I lie. "Don't worry about me."

"Hmm," she says, her eyes twinkling. "You get to share a bed with *Liam*. In his penthouse. And he looks at you like he's found buried treasure and he's just opened up the chest." Bailey laughs. "There are worse things in life."

I huff out a laugh but don't reply.

Does he?

"Get some sleep," I tell her.

She gets a shit-eating grin and wiggles her eyebrows at me. "You *too*." I groan and shut the door behind me. When I stand at the top of the stairs, Ben and Bailey safe behind me because of Liam, my emotions stir deep inside me. He's a good man. God, he's such a good man. And though I've only just begun to get to know him, every time I reveal another layer, I think I love him a little more.

"Cora," he calls in a playful tone when he sees me at the top of the stairs. "Are you gonna get your ass down here, or what?"

Biting my lip, I nod my head and go to him. When I first met this man, I couldn't imagine he had a playful side, but the way he calls to me it's as if he's beckoning me to come out and play.

I take a look at those huge windows, and for a moment, imagine what we could do in front of them. He sits on the couch, and hell if I don't love that disheveled look of his.

When his eyes take me in, I don't even try to hide the fact I'm staring at him, too. The way the fire flickers on his handsome features. His glass is empty, but he still holds it between his fingers, his eyes dancing with firelight. The knowing smirk he gives me tells me he's mentally undressing me, and hell, I'm okay with that. I agreed to this. And after tonight, I'm eager. But when I reach him, he just puts his wine glass down and reaches for me.

"Come here," says, his voice low and raspy in the quiet. "Want to get some sleep, sweetheart?"

"Well," I tell him. "Yes. But not until I've thanked you."

"Don't be silly," he says, dragging me onto his lap. "It was the least I could do."

A few weeks ago, I'd have protested sitting on his lap, but the first time I told him I was too heavy, he put a decided end to *that* by putting me belly-down over his lap. And now, I've grown used to how nice it feels sitting like a little girl like this on his lap. I lay my head on his chest and play with the top button on his shirt.

"Well, I mean, I guess," I tell him. "But you were under no obligation to take us all to your home. And I want to thank you."

Leaning down, he lifts my chin with the tip of his finger, then brushes his lips against mine before he drags them to my cheek and kisses me there, then my temple and forehead, so reverently it's like an act of worship.

"Do you?" he asks. "What exactly might that thank you entail?"

My body is already heating from being so close to the man who's commanded my body through pleasure and pain these past weeks, grows molten. I love being close to him like this, getting lost to the intimacy of our nearness. The rapid beating of his pulse. His signature scent, earthy and masculine like the burning embers of a fire in winter. The rasp of his voice and brush of his lips. Every detail strips away what's on my mind until I find the peace that comes in this closeness while my heart beats faster.

I want more than a kiss, and he knows it.

God, I'll miss this.

I whisper in his ear. "I think it's time I had a tour of your bedroom."

And then I'm in his arms and he's standing, walking toward his room. He needs no further prompting. My heartbeat races when he kisses me hungrily, tongue and teeth and lips and moans, and I'm drowning in this moment.

He carries me to his room. "Bedroom," he growls, kicking the door shut behind him. "Tour over. Get these fucking clothes off."

"Impatient, are we?" I murmur when he tosses me on the bed, but his only response is a sharp crack to the ass. He's taking his clothes off with impatient jerks and tugs.

"Get 'em off before I do, and if I do, you won't be wearing those again."

"Oooh," I tease, doing what he says and stripping quickly. "So brutal."

"I'll give you brutal, sweetheart." I'm scrambling belly-down on his massive bed and my timing sucks. He's just taken off his belt, which he wastes no time in doubling and smacking across my ass. I gasp, and before I can even take another breath, he strikes me again, and again, and I'm welcoming the perfect pain that I need tonight.

It hurts like fuck, but hell if I don't like the way the leather makes me throb. He's used every implement he owns on me, and affectionately calls me *leather whore* because every time he spanks me with leather, I ignite.

We're far enough away from Ben and Bailey with their doors closed and thank God for that, so I don't worry they can hear us.

"You need a taste of this, don't you?"

I nod, as he spanks my flesh with the leather. He'll leave his mark on me and tomorrow every time I move, I'll feel the reminder of his dominance. I love that he knows this is what I need. He whips me with the belt until I pass the threshold of pain, and as he whips me, the pain begins to fade. I'm sinking, engulfed into blissful awareness and sensation, every strike bringing me closer to the well of peace I crave. Somewhere in the distance I can still hear the swish and smack of the belt, his low commands to lie still and take it, but I'm fading into a blissful quiet of welcome relief. This is where he can take me, this chasm of brutal reprieve.

And then my mind grows quiet. The belt drops, and though my eyes are closed I can almost see him behind me. When his hands span my waist, I arch into him. I need him to fill me. Claim me. His mouth at my ear, he lines his cock at my entrance. It hurts, hell does it hurt, my bruised, punished flesh against his skin, but this is a pain that erases all other.

"Fucking beautiful," he growls with a thrust of his hips. I moan and brace for the savage friction and pleasure. When he wraps my hair in his fist in one fierce sweep of his hand, I don't fight it. I need this release. I need to lose control to him. I need his dominance. "My sweet, beautiful pain slut," he rasps in my ear. "My little leather whore."

"Yes, sir," I say with a grin and moan as he rocks his hips and my heartbeat races. I'm getting closer to climax and so is he, but this is no lover's dance or gentle dalliance, but carnal surrender. I moan low on the cusp of climax, then scream when he pulls my hair back so I arch my body against his.

"Come, Cora. Come, beautiful girl."

Ecstasy sweeps over me when I ride him, milking his cock with no reservation, my own release meeting his in silent perfection until we collapse together.

"Christ," he swears, mumbling under his breath, and I swear for one minute I hear him say *I love you*.

I'm suddenly sober.

"What?" I say. Drunk on pleasure, maybe I just imagined what I heard.

"I said 'God, I love that,'" he says, but he doesn't meet my eyes, and too soon, he's up and cleaning me off, then tucking me into bed. He rolls toward me and pulls me onto his chest. It's the first time we've slept in the same bed. I'll enjoy every second of this until it's gone.

I like being held in his arms. My heart swells with the closeness of our bodies and our synchronized breathing. I've never felt so cherished or safe.

If I say it out loud, it's a betrayal. I've broken a contract.

I can't say it out loud, but I sing it in my mind.

I love you, Liam Alexander. I may never get to tell you, but I will always love you.

EIGHTEEN

Liam

I CAN'T GET ENOUGH of her. Cora's a drug that's seeped into my veins, crawled under my skin, and tethered herself to me.

Her smile. Her laugh. Her wit and intellect and humor. I'm in danger of drowning with no life preserver in sight, and I don't fucking care.

I call her to my office the last week of our contract, and hell, I feel like time is ticking.

What happens when our contract ends?

Rule number six plays in my mind so often now, it's tormenting me.

Love?

Until Cora, the notion was preposterous, really. I barely even liked the women I contracted with much less loved them. But Cora... God, what she does to me. What she *gives* me.

After the night we made love in my bed, things changed between us. I think we both know it, but it's something we can't speak of.

I love having her in my home and hell, I love Ben and Bailey there, too. I liked being alone, but I love *not* being alone even more. I didn't know what I was missing until I had it. I'm teaching Ben basic chords on the piano, and Cora and Bailey are enjoying the hell out of living in my penthouse, with full access to the pool, the workout room, and the spa. And *I* enjoy the hell out of spoiling them.

We haven't talked about them moving out in the week they've been there. The last time we did, I told Cora I liked them here and made some kinda vague remark about one of my guys finding them a place to live. What I didn't tell her is that I threw out the printout he gave me with all the details.

Ben and Bailey enjoy getting rides to school, and Cora enjoys knowing they're safe. We still go to Verge, but more and more I'm spending time in the penthouse I once viewed as little more than a place to crash. It's the first time it's ever felt like... home.

And I've never felt at home. Not when I lived with my parents. Not when I lived in a boarding-house. It isn't until they're all there that I realize I've been a sort of nomad. It's an interesting concept to grapple with, but I'm happy where I am.

She doesn't hold back with me anymore, and

hell if she isn't everything I've ever wanted. Our contract is almost up, but I don't care. I think I know what I'll do when it's up. I'll pay her in full and...

No. The truth is, I have no idea what I'll do.

It depends on her, really.

She has school today, but no shift at the bookstore, and I'm making good use of the time we have together.

I want you in here at eight, dressed in the simplest clothing you can so I can take it off you when you get here.

Yes, sir.

I can almost see those eyes of hers light up as she bites her lip and looks through her clothing. The way her pulse races and she shifts on her feet at the knowledge that she'll be in my office today to do with what I please.

Will you use me, sir?

The text makes me smile.

In every possible way.

We've spent every damn day together since that night in Verge when she was first mine.

I've scened with so many women, one might call me proficient in the art of BDSM. But punishment... real discipline... it did something to Cora. There was more than the physical exchange of power that night, and neither one of us could have predicted what it did to her. To *us*.

I knew the cane would be difficult for her. I had no idea that my punishment would break her open the way it did, and I had not the slightest inkling of how I'd want to put her back together again. Something happened that night, but I won't let myself think about the ramifications. We have a contract. This is an agreement between two people, friends with fucking first class benefits, and I told myself I'm strong enough not to fall for her.

I lied.

Jesus fucking Christ, though. It would take a will of iron to resist a woman like Cora. She's the whole fucking deal. Brilliant. Stunning. And the scenes... *Christ,* she's the perfect sub. If she has a hard limit, I haven't found it yet, though she still shakes a little when we dabble in wax. Every time I bring her to the edge of fear, she climaxes harder than she ever has before.

We've explored the depths of Verge and we've only just begun.

I didn't plan for this to happen, but here we are, and I have no intention of letting her go. When the contract is up... I'll have to make her another offer.

I haven't yet worked out the details of how I'll handle this.

I focus hard on the work I have to do before she arrives and lose track of the time. I've given Mandy the day off, so Cora and I have a bit more freedom than we normally do, and Manuel announces their arrival shortly after eight thirty. I frown at the time. They were supposed to be here earlier, and it's unlike them not to arrive promptly.

I punch a button my phone and ask him, "Why so late?"

"She wasn't ready when I arrived, sir," he says, then quickly amends, "but she got ready as fast as she could, and we might have hit a little traffic on the way."

Is he covering for her? I frown. "Might have hit a little traffic?" Traffic in NYC is brutal, but a quick glance at my monitor shows me the distance to my office is no worse than usual.

"Yes, sir," he says.

"Very well. Send her up."

"I'm already here," comes a voice on the other side of the door.

"Come in." I push the button to allow her entrance to my office, leaning back in my chair so I can watch her enter. She lights up a room when she comes in, and I want to see the transformation, but I'm not quite sure what happened with my instructions this morning.

The door opens, and Cora stands in the entryway, the light of the hall behind her casting her body in shadow so I can't quite see.

"Shut the door," I command. "And stay right there."

The door clicks shut and now I can see her fully, dressed in a little dress we picked up last week for her, a casual, hunter green number that dips to a low vee in front, that I know from personal experience simply slips on and off, with no fussy buttons or zippers or ties to deal with, so it can be removed in record time. An important point.

But first, we have something to discuss.

"Why were you late?" I demand, fixing her with the stern glare that usually makes her humble and contrite.

"I... well..." she begins, and though I've trained her to keep her eyes on mine when I speak to her, she looks away.

"Cora," I warn, but she doesn't look at me.

"I overslept," she says, but by the way she shifts her feet and won't meet my eyes, I can tell she isn't telling the truth. She's lying to me? Being late earns a minor consequence, but a lie?

I can't abide lying.

I'll have an answer.

"Look at me."

She swivels her gaze to mine and there's fire in her eyes. I get to my feet, prepared to meet that challenge. This is an exchange of power she's agreed to and here, right now, in this room, she needs a reminder. I need to strip away whatever's holding her back from submitting to me, and everything about her right now from her stature to her tone, to the way her eyes harden when she looks at me, says she isn't prepared to submit.

Has this all been an act? Has she feigned submission, and now that we're near the end of the contract, she's putting up a wall?

Our contract isn't up yet, and I'll fucking remind her of that.

I snap my fingers and point to the carpeted floor.

"Knees."

Well trained, she falls to her knees in obedience, though her eyes still spark defiance.

I crook my finger at her and give a silent command.

Crawl.

With a sharp intake of breath and pinched lips, she hesitates. I do a mental calculation of what I have at my disposal in my office. Though I'm discreet, I'm fairly well outfitted for play here, and I know in the other room I used to have a stout riding crop, but I think I've brought all the other tools to Verge.

The belt I'm wearing is well-crafted Italian leather.

It will do.

One foot forward. Then two. She's crawling toward me reluctantly, her eyes alight in anger. I don't know what it is that's gotten under her skin, but I will.

I wait, watching to see if her anger bleeds off as she comes to me on all fours, but it seems the closer she gets, the angrier she becomes, until she's at my feet all but glaring at me. I drop to one knee and chuck a finger under her chin.

"This is no submissive woman I have kneeling before me," I say. "You began our day with disobedience, and now everything about you speaks defiance. What is it?"

"Nothing, sir," she grits out.

I bring my fingers to her hair, and allow myself one stroke of the soft, silky strands, before I wrap them in my fingers and tug her head back, hard. Punishing. "That's a lie."

Her eyes water from the hair pull, but her mouth is clamped shut.

I could bend her over my desk and take my belt to her ass and attempt to whip the truth out of her. Or I could stand her in the corner until she finally caves and tells me. I have many options at my disposal, but instead of immediate punishment, I decide to give myself time to think about it while I make her submit. Sometimes the actual act of physical submission is what it takes.

"Alright, then," I say, getting to my feet but holding her hair so she hisses and scrambles to her feet beside me. "Since you won't open your mouth to speak the truth, let's put that mouth to better use, shall we?" She swallows but remains silent.

Hell, I've got work to do. She can do her work while I do mine.

I release her hair and take her hand, leading her to the large desk. I sit at my chair and stand her in front of me. In one quick tug, I divest her of her dress, pleased to see she wears a simple bra and no panties. Soon, she stands naked before me. The large windows behind me showcase the heart of NYC, but the glass is mirrored, so though we can see every high rise and taxi cab below, no one can see us. It gives me the illusion of transparency but the security of privacy all at once.

But Cora doesn't know that.

"Under my desk," I instruct. "On your knees."

She obeys but reluctantly, falling to her knees in front of me with flashing eyes. I open my desk drawer and remove a few items that will help me prepare her. They clink onto the glass-covered desk, and for the first time since she's come in here, her eyes register surprise, widening ever so slightly and her lips soften.

First, the handcuffs. I'm prepared for this, and have already placed everything I need in my desk. I bend down and bring her wrists behind her back, before I click the metal in place. I make sure they're secure but only slightly uncomfortable, enough to make her know her place but not too much to cause distress. With her hands fastened behind her back, she kneels with legs spread apart and back arched, as she's been taught. Next comes the silk blindfold I slide over her eyes and tie behind her head. With her vision and movement impaired, she takes in a deep breath. The first layer of resistance strips away.

Next, I open the lubricant, squeeze some onto my hand, and glide it over her ass, making sure I lubricate her asshole good and well.

"Liam," she whispers. The angry little girl who stepped foot in my office a few minutes ago is almost gone.

"Cora," I respond.

"What is that? I mean, I know what it is, but what are you—ooooh, oh my God—"

Suddenly she knows exactly what it is, as I guide the lubricated plug into her ass.

It's a stubborn sub who can maintain anger and defiance when she's cuffed, blindfolded, and plugged, kneeling on her feet in front of me.

The only freedom she has right now is speech, and soon I'll strip that away from her, too. When she hears the clink of my belt buckle, she freezes.

Good. I wasn't planning on strapping her yet, and my range of motion is limited with her sitting in front of me, but I double the belt and give her a good crack across the ass. She hisses and squirms, but I can still feel whatever angers her emanating her like heat from embers. I'll draw this out of her, but sometimes it takes a bit of finesse. Dropping my belt to the floor, I unzip my pants and slide out my cock, already hard, into my hand. Shifting my chair closer to her, I slide my cock to her full lips.

"Open."

Her lips part and I take a deep breath. She's fucking good at this.

I push my hips toward her and slide my cock into her mouth, stifling a groan when her tongue circles the head.

"Naughty little girls who don't tell the truth get punished," I tell her. "You've lost your sight and movement, and now instead of what I planned, you can service me under my desk while I work. Understood?"

I tug her head bag to make her nod, then pump my hips. She chokes a little, and I pump harder. When she sucks in breath around my cock, she builds suction. I stifle a groan. She won't know she's affected me, not this time. I sit up straighter and turn my attention to my desk, opening up my email while she works her mouth on my dick. I click my keyboard while she sucks, and answer a call that comes in, my voice unaffected by what she's doing.

Hell, she's fucking working me to distraction, but I want her to feel this, to know she can come in here wearing that anger like a cloak, but I'll strip that veil away and bring her to her knees.

It's where she's happy, though. Submitting to me comes as naturally to her as blinking her eyes, intuitive and instinctual, her visceral reaction to my dominance a beautiful sight to see. But sometimes, she needs a little help to get there.

My phone blinks yellow. I groan. Jake's line.

I pump my hips, making her gag and squirm. "Suck it," I order, right before I slam the button on my phone.

"Liam, we've got to talk," he says. "The damn news picked up that story of those college kids."

Is this what's on her mind?

"Jesus, Jake, so you have nothing better to do with your time than follow this story? It doesn't matter. We've got groundbreaking sales in Milwaukee, we're on the verge of breaking new ground overseas, and the damn White House is interested in buying vacation homes in the Keys, and you're still harping on about the goddamn protest those kids are doing?"

Cora freezes, but a sharp tug to her hair makes her suck again with renewed vigor. I thrust into her hard enough she gags, then continues energetically.

"Yes," he says. "You have no idea how this negative publicity can affect your name, Liam."

At least I think that's what he says. I'm not as focused as I usually am, for obvious reasons.

I pump harder into her mouth, getting closer and closer to release, and fuck if she isn't going to suck every damn drop.

"I don't give a fuck," I tell him, ending on a barely-contained groan. "I gotta go."

"I'm coming up," he says. "You've got papers to sign, and they're vital."

I groan out loud this time, getting closer and closer to coming. "Fine," I tell him. He'll think I just don't want to deal with him, which is usually the case. "Get up here."

"I'm in the building. I'll be there in a minute."

Shit. I figured he wasn't anywhere near this close.

I end the call and grip my desk just as I climax, my seed spurting down her throat, but like the good sub she is, she sucks and swallows and doesn't miss a beat until she's taken every damn drop. I give myself just a few seconds to slump against my desk before I groan and push back my seat. Jake's coming up and I want her out from under my desk.

I remove my cock from her perfect mouth with

a groan and quickly dress, then lean toward her and cup her jaw. "Good girl," I say, removing her blind-fold. Her eyes are no longer fiery and raw but bright with arousal, and when I release her cuffs, her hands swing free, coming to rest on my lap.

"A little of that fight's gone out of you?" I ask, lifting her chin. She nods. I want to find out what's on her mind and read her heart, but we have no time. I reach down and cup her perfect breast in my palm, then guide my hand to her ass and remove the plug. She comes up on her toes and I pat her ass.

God, I wish we had more time. "You behave yourself today, and I'll reward you tonight, Cora."

She bites her lip and whispers, "Yes, sir. Liam, really, I'm sorry. It wasn't *you.*"

"Have you learned your lesson about taking it out on your dom?"

Chastened, she nods, but I lean in and kiss her soft, damp temple, tucking a tendril of vibrant hair behind her ear. "Listen, baby," I tell her. "I can take you. You know that? You bring whatever's pissing you off to me, and I'll help you. But first, you've got to talk to me. I'm not a damn mind reader."

She huffs out a mirthless laugh. "I'm not so sure about that sometimes." There's no denying the power exchange has given me a window into her mind and heart.

"We'll talk about what's going on in a few minutes. For now, go into the other room and rest while you wait for me."

Subdued, chastened, she stands, and if I know Cora, she's intensely aroused. Sometimes having to wait can keep her submissive, though today my preference would be to make her come over my desk. She gathers up her dress and steps quickly into the other room, shutting and locking the door behind her just as Jake knocks on the door.

I right myself and open my computer, feigning indifference as I tell him to come in. I want to get rid of him as quickly as I possibly can, because I need to see to Cora.

Jake comes into the room with a stack of papers he slams on my desk, his cheeks bright with fury.

"Jesus, man," I say, rolling my eyes. "Will you get a grip? Why do you let a couple of college students get under your skin like this?"

"Couple of college students?" he says, pointing a chubby, sausage-like finger at the headline on the paper. "Their Instagram protest's gone viral, Liam. *Viral.*"

"Honest to God, Jake, I have no idea what you're talking about," I tell him. I sign a digital contract that's waiting in my inbox, agree to an interview in a West Coast entrepreneurial magazine, and push the buttons that light up on my phone to voicemail. Shit, days when I give Mandy off don't always work so well.

"What the hell is your problem?" I tell him.

"Liam," he says, "Christ. Look at me!"

This is the last damn time this guy's giving me an order.

"Jake," I tell him, my eyes on my screen. "You may have been on my payroll for a solid decade, but I'm telling you now, you tell me what to do again, and I'll fire your ass."

"Please," he says, pleading. "You hired me to tell you what to do. And I made that contract for you. I know you're with that girl who's spearheading this."

A choked sound comes from the other room, but if he hears it, he doesn't react.

"She's an instigator," he mutters.

I swivel to look at him and clench my jaw to stop from hauling him by the fucking collar over my desk. I take in a deep breath then let it out slowly. This guy is on my last damn nerve. I'm closing this deal that's pending, then having Mandy scout another lawyer next week. I'm done with his bullshit.

"I do *not* hire you to *tell me what to do,*" I say, my voice tight with anger. "I hire you to defend me in court when necessary. I know what to do. What I do not know is the ins and outs of the legal system." He opens his mouth then closes it and sighs, but I have the distinct feeling his attitude is fake, and he's simmering hot under that collar.

"Sorry," he says. "But I'm worried about the ramifications of this."

"Why? Who the hell cares?"

"*I* care," he says, slamming his finger on the paper, and I finally look at the headline. When I do,

I feel like someone's just dumped a bucket of ice water down my chest.

It's a picture of a pink square thing that says *Instagrammer on Crusade Against Big Business*, and beside the image is a picture of Cora.

Jesus.

Did this have anything to do with why she stormed into my office this morning?

I grab the paper out of Jake's fat hands and spread it out to read it.

LAST NIGHT AT MIDNIGHT, college student Cora Myers began an online petition that went viral. Protesting what she calls "Wall Street's Pompous Elite," Myers and half a dozen of her environmentalist counterparts filed a complaint last month with the New York City Counsel of Ecological Advancement and Agriculture, but a judge dismissed their petition before it went to court. Undeterred, Myers and her friends decided to take it a step further than court and brought their axes to grind on social media.

I CONTINUE READING the article in stunned silence. I told her to continue her crusade, because I didn't want her fight to interfere with our relationship. But this still takes me by surprise.

Last night at ten o'clock, she was trussed up in the navy room at Verge, my rope criss-crossing under her breasts and thighs like she was a present under the Christmas tree, before I fingered her pussy and fucked her ass. She came harder than I've ever seen her come and passed out in my bed.

According to this paper, she put this petition up an hour later?

If the papers knew anything about our personal relationship...

Jesus.

"Well, I don't know what they can really do," I tell him. "The deal is all but signed."

"All *but signed,*" Jake says. "For Christ's sake, Liam. Aren't you listening at all?"

I don't respond because I'm trying to prevent myself from breaking his goddamn nose.

"They're preventing the signing. This petition's gotten the attention of the most prominent public figures, and they're trying to put an end to this."

I don't give a shit about paving the fucking Greenery.

I do give a shit that she posted this online right after I fucked her perfect little ass.

"On what grounds?" I ask him. "It's a solid deal."

"On the grounds of the physical health of the city's citizens," he says, rolling his eyes. "This girl has stepped in where she doesn't belong despite your contract."

"The contract is almost up," I tell him, trying to end this discussion. "And anyway, the truth is, it's void anyway. Screw the contract."

It could be my imagination, but I think I hear a sound in the other room.

"Good. I thought you'd come to your senses," he says. "So she's a non-issue."

He doesn't know how I've wrestled with this. Non-issue? *Ha.*

It's everything else that's become a *non-issue.*

I clench my hands under the desk. God, how satisfying would it be to deck him. Yeah, she's made my job infinitely harder and I want answers, but that doesn't give him the right to say a damn thing against her.

He sighs and shakes his head. "Still, I'm not sure I can stop this, Liam."

"Good. Don't."

He blinks and gets to his feet, his red face turning purple. "So, you're really going to just let this slutty girl come into your life and wreck things?"

I get to my feet and plant my hands on the desk to prevent myself from breaking his nose. Assaulting a lawyer like him would not be good. "Wreck things?" I ask in a deadly calm voice that belies the fury that rips through me. Hell, she hasn't wrecked anything. She's fixed what I didn't even know was broken. "Get out," I order. "I expect your resignation by noon. Drop the case, and invoice me for your time."

Still purple in the face, he suddenly realizes I'm firing him. "You're—you can't—Liam, for God's sake," he goes on.

"Get. *Out.*"

I wait until he's gone, cursing myself for giving Mandy the day off. I want her canceling my meetings for the rest of the day and checking security footage to make sure Jake's truly out of here. I spend about ten minutes flipping through email. I want this off my plate before I discuss things with Cora.

"Cora?" I call out. "Get in here. I need to talk to you."

No response. If she's going silent on me now...

We need to talk. This is not the time for her to clam up.

"Cora?"

I walk into the other room and come to a halt a few steps in but I can't see her. Hell, she's nowhere to be found and there aren't many places to hide in here. The door's left open.

Jesus.

She's gone. I can't believe she left like this, so soon.

I stand and shake my head. I warned her. I thought I'd subdued her and broken through, but maybe she *does* need a session with leather.

"Cora?" I call, but there's no response. I can't believe she took off without even talking to me and hell, we have shit to talk about. After all this time, she'd run?

I go back to my office and pick up my phone, scowling at it. I've been too easy on her. We've scened, and she knows what I expect, but she's never really earned herself a proper punishment since that brief caning when we first began. Tonight, we'll have a good talk about running.

With my belt.

I call her, but it immediately goes to voicemail. I send a text and I'm not surprised when I don't get a response.

You do not ignore my calls and texts. You know better than this.

My phone sits, mute. I try to think of where she'd be right now, so I call Manuel.

"Where's Cora?"

"School, sir. She's at her morning class," he says, though his voice is hard and distant, and this is not the easygoing person who works for me.

"I'll be right down. Take me to her." I don't bother to listen to his reply. I'm already heading downstairs.

NINETEEN

Cora

GOD, I've fucked everything up. When I heard his lawyer tell him how I'd messed up his deal, and Liam said the contract was void... I couldn't listen for another minute. He must know I've fallen in love with him and breached the contract.

I had to get to school and make this better. He isn't the man I thought he was.

He's so much more. So much better.

And he doesn't deserve a girl like me, who doesn't have two pennies to scrape together. We're four days away from ending the contract, and for a moment there, I actually convinced myself that maybe we'd transcended the ridiculous agreement we signed weeks ago. That I meant something more to him than a hard fuck. But how could I? He's so out of my league we're not even in the same stratosphere. I need to get that damn petition taken down and stop making a mess of Liam's life.

I came into his office this morning fuming because someone had put the petition on my Instagram page without my permission, and we didn't get a chance to even talk about it.

I almost skipped the ride to school today, but when I got downstairs, the sky had turned a dismal, ominous gray. I slid into the car just before the skies opened and rain slashed down in torrents. Manuel asked no questions but took me straight to school.

"I'll get myself home today," I told him, and he didn't much like that idea. But I insisted.

"It's been great getting to you know," I tell him, which sounds super lame, but I have to say good-bye. "Thank you for everything."

He looks at me curiously, then frowns at the torrential downpour out the window.

"Are you going to be okay?" he asks.

No. Hell, no, I'm not going to be okay. I fell in love with a man I cannot have. I dragged my brother and sister through this, and now I need to end it. Say good-bye. But I know Manuel is only talking about the rain, so I lie.

"I'll be fine but thank you." And I leave before he can say another word.

I head to the journalism office first, because I want answers. Someone put a petition up on my page, and that someone was not me. The rain beats down on me in cold sheets as I run to the office, and I can almost hear Liam chiding me for letting myself get cold and wet. But what does it matter? I push the door open and slam it behind me. Four wide sets of eyes blink up at me. I don't even bother with formalities.

"Who the hell put up a petition on my page without my consent?"

A tall, thin girl with scraggly blonde hair piled high on her head lifts a tentative hand. "Um, me," she says. "Did you forget that you gave me access to your social media?"

"Access to my social media," I repeat. "I thought you were going to manage the pictures from the Greenery. I had no idea you'd be putting up a viral petition like that."

"But it was such a success!" she argues. "We've gotten the attention of the local news, and they're coming to interview us in an hour."

"Take it down."

"What? Cora!"

But I'm mad as hell and I've got something to say about this. "Take it fucking *down*. And don't ever put anything else up like that on my page again."

Rising to her full height, she shoots me a look of fury. "Fine. I'll take it down. Will I take this as your resignation from the protest team?" I almost laugh out loud. It seems so foolish in comparison to what I've faced these past weeks.

"Yes," I tell her.

God, I've messed everything up. Bailey and Ben are homeless and living on Liam's charity.

Liam's lawyer is furious because of me. I have to get Ben and Bailey and their things. We have little left after the fire, but it's time to move out of Liam's penthouse. I'm walking in the rain, cold and wet and alone, not even realizing where I'm going until I see the welcome sign for The Greenery. With a sigh, I stroll through the gardens.

Though the summer blossoms have faded, before me lies rows and rows of vibrant mums heralding the advent of winter. I reach out and touch one fiery orange blossom with the tip of my finger.

"They're hardy, strong flowers." My heart squeezes at the sound of his voice.

I don't turn to look at him, but nod. "They are," I agree. "They don't cower when the winds come or wilt under hard rain, because they're made to withstand the cold that's coming." I take in a deep breath and remember why I came here, why any of this matters to me at all. Eight weeks ago, this had me fired up, but now... but now, I have bigger things to worry about. Ben and his book reports and science projects. Bailey and all that she's got in front her still, years of high school then finding her way in this world. Where we'll live, where they can go to school. I want out of NYC. I want something new, a change, and now that I've got money in the bank, I'm going to do this for them.

And me. I need to take care of *me*.

"How did you find me?" I ask, still not turning

around. I don't want to see the sapphire eyes, because if I do, I don't trust that I can stay strong.

"Tracked you like a stalker," he says, coming in front of me and holding up his phone. "Remember?"

"Oh," I say with a sigh. "Right."

"Liam, I... I can't do this," I tell him. My voice feels tight and strange, when I bring my eyes up to his. "I know we are at the end of this contract, and I've been asking myself for weeks what that will mean. Because I don't want to see it end." I close my eyes and take a deep breath, steeling myself for what I need to say. "I am moving out. I'm taking my things and Ben and Bailey's. I've made a mess of things and I don't want to do this anymore."

The look in his eyes makes my heart ache, and for a moment, I let myself believe that I'm more than someone he contracted.

He won't listen to excuses or reason, so I have to give him something that he *will* listen to. He takes a step toward me, and I shake my head, holding up my palm to him. "It's time for us to end this. I broke the contract. You owe me nothing." I shake my head, swallowing back tears that threaten to fall. "You need to let me go." I lift my chin. "Like you said earlier, our contract is almost up."

I don't know how to handle the fact that he stands there in silence with his fists clenched, like he doesn't know what to do or say. I have to go. I can't stay here any longer, because every second in his presence makes me lose a bit of my resolve.

"You can't break the contract," he says. "You promised me."

"What does that even mean?" I tell him, heat rising in my chest at what his damn lawyer said. I knew it. One look in those blue depths and my resolve begins to dwindle. I have to push him away. "*You* were the one who told your lawyer it didn't matter because the contract was void. Then fine. Rip it up."

I turn away from him. I can't take this anymore.

It's over. God, I have to get away from him because if he touches me...

When he reaches for my arm, I close my eyes.

"You can't touch me," I whisper. "I need to walk away and you're making it impossible."

"So that's what it's about," he says, pulling me to him. The rain falls harder, blurring my vision, running down my face in rivulets with my tears. "You jumped to conclusions."

I try to pull away from him. I can't stand it one more minute.

"Cora, you listen to me," he says, grabbing me about the shoulders and shaking me. "*Listen.* The contract is void because *I* broke it. Not *you.* Rule number six," he says, dragging me to his chest, we're both soaked through to the skin. A flash of lightning overhead lights up the sky and I see his eyes look down on me with a tenderness that gives me pause.

Wait. *What?*

"I love you," he says through the rain, cupping

my face in his palm and pulling me closer. "I love you. And I won't let you get away from me. Not now. Not ever."

Then his mouth is on mine as lightning splits the sky in two.

"Come home with me," he says. "Get in the car and let's go. Let's drive away. We'll buy a house in the country and take Ben and Bailey and leave this all behind. They can keep the Greenery and I can build somewhere else, because I don't care. None of that matters. This is all that does."

"We both broke rule number six," I tell him. "I thought you knew."

"Knew what?"

"That I love *you,*" I tell him. "God, we're a pair of saps declaring love amid the flowers in a damn rain storm."

Chuckling, he pulls me to his sodden chest again. "Don't you ever run from me again," he warns.

"I'm sorry," I tell him, then give him a little fake pout. "I should maybe be... punished?"

His growl makes my body heat despite the freezing rain. "You sound a little too eager," he says.

"No contract," I muse. "Does that mean I have no rules? No consequences for disobedience?"

"Like hell," he rasps out, pinching my ass.

And all is right with the world.

EPILOGUE

"I'LL MISS THE CROWDS," Bailey says. We're in the back of Liam's car, and the four of us are moving the hell out of NYC. "And the stores."

"I'll miss the cheesecake," Ben says with a wistful sigh. "And the pizza."

"You guys, it's not like we're never coming back here," I tell them. "Right, Liam?"

"Of course not," he says, ruffling Ben's hair and tugging a lock of Bailey's. They both grin, and my heart melts a little. God, I love how he is with them. For the man who never wanted children or to be saddled with responsibilities, he's taken to a ready-made-family as if it were meant to be.

And maybe it was.

"But I'll tell ya, after you eat *real* pizza in Italy and real pastry in France, you may never want to come back to New York again."

He's bought a place an hour from the heart of the city, and he's promised me we'll return. After all, we have a private room at Verge, and I don't want to miss my friends. I'm oh so happy to get out of the city, though.

"Oh my God, I want to go to Italy," Bailey says. "And Paris!"

"Well, good," I tell them. "Because someone's splurged on a graduation present for me, and we all get to go."

Ben's eyes widen comically and Bailey squeals. "Oh my God, Liam, I love you! Well, you know, not the way *she* loves you," she says, chattering on with the pink-cheeked blush that seems to run in the family. "I love you like a brother, and you know, that's what you'll be once you two... You know."

He looks at me and I look at him, and I feel a lump rise in my throat. I do know.

"You two gettin' hitched?" Ben asks curiously, his head tipped to the side.

"Ben!" Bailey says, smacking his arm.

"I dunno," Liam says. "Depends on whether or not your sister will have me." We cruise to a stop when we pull up outside of our new house.

I look from Liam to Ben to Bailey and all of a sudden they're grinning, all of them, and Liam's pulling a black velvet box out of his pocket.

"They were in on this, too," he says. "I thought it would be all poetic justice if I proposed during the ribbon-cutting ceremony at the new botanical garden, but you know..." His voice grows husky as he turns to me. "Get out of the damn car so I can get on one knee."

"So romantic," I tease, but I think I fly out of the car. He takes my hand and practically drags me out. The sun is shining and birds twitter in the air above us as if nature itself rejoices in this moment.

Liam drops to one knee and meets my eyes, suddenly sober.

"Cora, I love you," he says. I want to capture this moment. I want to hold it in my heart and cherish it forever. My eyes fill with tears when he asks me. "Will you marry me? Until death do us part and all that—"

But I'm already tackling him to the ground and throwing my arms around him. "Hell, yes I'll marry you," I tell him. Bailey and Ben whoop and holler as he slips the ring on my finger, then Bailey takes Ben and drags him away when he pulls me to him for a kiss.

"A private ceremony," I whisper, when I'm up against his chest. "With no damn media coverage."

"Absolutely," he says. "Let's get married in Italy, after you graduate."

"Oh, I love how you think," I tell him. "But what about... I thought you didn't want a family. Are you sure this is what you want for forever?" I ask, watching Ben and Bailey run ahead to check out the new house. It's big and spacious and has a yard. They'll each have their own room, and I'm on the first floor with Liam.

He shrugs. "They're not exactly babies," he says. "But hell, I like having them around." He's suddenly shy, an unusual look on him. "You know, I never had anything like this. And I like it."

"I more than like it," I tell him, holding his hand. "I love it, and I love you."

"I love you, too, baby." Leaning down, he kisses me. "You know, I've had this place already furnished."

"Oh?" I ask him curiously. "How so?"

He grins. "Wait until you see the master bedroom."

"Realllly," I say, curious as all hell.

"Let's just say I put a new spin on *master.*"

My heart trips in my chest. "Did you?"

He nods. "Manuel said he'd take Bailey and Ben to get some ice cream while we get the place... situated."

"Oh, you did think of everything, didn't you?"

Grinning, he pulls me to him for another kiss. "Wait until you see."

"I trust you," I tell him, my nose getting all tingly again. "I think it's the first time in my life I've ever said that."

He kisses me fully, and when he lets me go, the sapphire depths of his eyes burn into mine. "I know baby." Then he grins. "But maybe wait until you see the master bedroom..."

THE END

NEED MORE NYC DOMS?

Nyc Doms

Although each book is a stand-alone novel and can be read in any order, the chronological order is as follows:

Deliverance

He's bred to protect.

Tobias Creed likes things done his way, and he likes his women ready to submit. No strings attached. Until the night he meets the one woman who challenges him, practically begging to be taken over his knee.

As a single mom to a child with special needs, Diana McAdams does things her way. She's in control and doesn't have time for love. Happily-ever-afters aren't for her.

Then she meets the man who demands her submission...

Read more

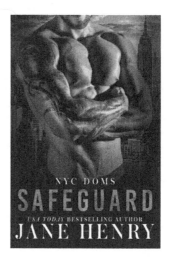

Safeguard

She's feisty, gorgeous, impossible.
Submissive.
And all mine.

I don't do half-assed relationships. When I set my sights on the most headstrong, tenacious submissive I've ever met, I'm all in. I'll show her the dark, sensual world she craves, dominate her, and leave her begging for more. But when her safety's endangered, she needs more than a dom: she needs a safeguard.

Read more

Conviction

Braxton Cannon can't get the girl on the dance floor out of his mind, the woman he literally swept off her feet and into Club Verge.

She's no submissive, but he can't help but admire her ferocity, even as he yearns to take her over his lap and teach her manners. He's determined to keep her safe if he has to lock her up himself.

Officer Zoe Mackay can handle herself. But when she learns information that puts her life at risk, she's forced to seek the assistance of a private investigator. Little does she know the man she hires is none other than Braxton Cannon, the high-handed dominant who gave her the hottest one-night stand of her life. With her assailants in hot pursuit, Zoe is forced to seek refuge in Club Verge, where she finds way more than she's bargained for...

Read more

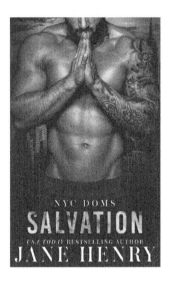

Salvation

Seven years ago, she was sheltered. In need of guidance. I was a newly-ordained priest with a vow of celibacy. Our love affair was torrid, and wrong, and ended in heartbreak.

We broke it off and went our separate ways.

I left the priesthood. She left her home.

Seven years later, she's stranded in my NYC Club while a blizzard rages outside, and she wants a taste of dominance.

I won't let another man lay eyes on her, much less touch her.

She's still my everything. My salvation.

And there's no way I'm letting her go...

Read more...

ABOUT THE AUTHOR

USA Today bestselling author Jane Henry pens stern but loving alpha heroes, feisty heroines, and emotion-driven happily-ever-afters. She writes what she loves to read: kink with a tender touch. Jane is a hopeless romantic who lives on the East Coast with a houseful of children and her very own Prince Charming.

What to read next? Here are some other titles by Jane you may enjoy. And don't forget to sign-up for my newsletter for a free book!

Contemporary fiction

Dark romance
   Island Captive: A Dark Romance

Undercover Doms standalones
   Criminal by Jane Henry and Loki Renard
   Hard Time by Jane Henry and Loki Renard

Wicked Doms
The Bratva's Baby

NYC Doms standalones

Deliverance
Safeguard
Conviction

Masters of Manhattan

Knave
Hustler

The Billionaire Daddies

Beauty's Daddy: A Beauty and the Beast Adult
Fairy Tale
Mafia Daddy: A Cinderella Adult Fairy Tale
Dungeon Daddy: A Rapunzel Adult Fairy Tale
The Billionaire Daddies boxset

The Boston Doms
My Dom (Boston Doms Book 1)
His Submissive (Boston Doms Book 2)
Her Protector (Boston Doms Book 3)
His Babygirl (Boston Doms Book 4)
His Lady (Boston Doms Book 5)
Her Hero (Boston Doms Book 6)
My Redemption (Boston Doms Book 7)

And more! Check out my Amazon author page.

You can find Jane here!

The Club (Facebook reader group)

Website

Amazon author page

Goodreads

Author Facebook page

Twitter handle: @janehenryauthor

Instagram

Made in the USA
Columbia, SC
10 May 2019